Losing Cotton

a novel

Losing Cotton

a novel

J.B. Hogan

TIREE
PRESS

an imprint of
OGHMA CREATIVE MEDIA

OGHMA

CREATIVE MEDIA

Tiree Press
An imprint of Oghma Creative Media, Inc.
2401 Beth Lane, Bentonville, Arkansas 72712

Library of Congress Cataloging-in-Publication Data

Names: Hogan, J.B., author.
Title: Losing Cotton/J.B. Hogan |
Description: Second Edition. | Bentonville: Tiree, 2019.
Identifiers: LCCN: 2018953880 | ISBN: 978-1-63373-476-0 (hardcover) |
ISBN: 978-1-63373-477-7 (trade paperback) | ISBN: 978-1-63373-478-4 (eBook)
Subjects: BISAC: FICTION/Historical | FICTION/Literary |
FICTION/Coming of Age
LC record available at: https://lccn.loc.gov/2018953880

Tiree Press trade paperback edition, March, 2019

Jacket & Interior Design by Casey W. Cowan
Editing by Gil Miller

Thanks to Casey Cowan for this incredible book cover and layout, and to Gordon Bonnet for his highly skilled and professional editing.

Losing
Cotton

a novel

1

S O, I GUESS YOU GUYS heard Richard Nixon's coming to Cotton." Jimmy Cates propped his lanky frame against the low wall of Manny Ruiz's Grocery Store parking lot. "What do you think of that?"

"That's pure bull." Shreve West lifted himself up onto the wall with the athletic ease that made him a star linebacker for the Cotton High School Boll Weevils. "Where do you get this crap? Nixon wouldn't be caught dead in Cotton. Hell, he wouldn't even go to El Centro, much less here. This ain't even a town, is it, Frank?"

Frank Mason leaned out from the wall and gave Main Street the once-over. Maybe eight or nine small businesses on each side and those separated by the highway that ran north to Indio and south to Mexico. Next to Ruiz's market was the post office where Frank and his mother lived in an upstairs apartment, and then the old drug store and soda fountain on the corner. Across the highway was the decaying hotel, a chunk of bricks missing from one wall when a northbound semi truck turned too sharp a few years back.

On down the street to the east were a couple of small stores and Chuy's pool hall—it was here all the local boys learned to shoot eight-ball and managed to sneak an occasional underage beer. Next to Chuy's was York's Electric, a parts and service store where Frank's mom worked, then Dale Honeycutt's barber shop, and finally Jackson's Cafe, the only place in town resembling a restaurant. For finer dining, there were towns to the south like Brawley, Imperial, or all the way to El Centro, but seldom as far as Calexico.

Opposite the boys was the bank, the Valley Hardware store, Doc Webster's office, and the weekly paper, *The Cotton Picker*. On the southeast corner of Main and the highway was a filling station where Lar Turner or one of the other three cops sat most of the time waiting for some driver to run the four-way stop sign. It had been erected to slow the big produce hauling rigs that rumbled in and out of town with their loads of lettuce, sugar beets, onions, and tomatoes.

Down from the station were a couple more general stores and a large grocery threatening to drive Manny Ruiz out of business. Last was the mechanic shop. Past it, scrub desert and empty, sandy fields led to the railroad tracks and big grain elevators. The tracks divided the central part of Cotton—downtown and the mostly white residential areas—from the Mexican and poor white migrant worker housing and a small settlement of blacks. The latter two areas were separated one from the other by the east-west road coming into or leaving Cotton.

Frank Mason finished his appraisal of downtown and tried to picture Richard Nixon visiting Cotton. He had to admit that it didn't seem likely.

"Don't seem likely to me." His southern twang was still strong even after two years in southern California. "Besides, why would he come now? He already lost the governor election. There wouldn't be no reason."

"Yeah." Shreve was impressed as usual with Frank's knowledge of current affairs. "What do you say to that, huh, Jimmy?" He reached behind Frank and slugged Cates. Cates cringed and rubbed his shoulder.

"Oww," he groaned, "darn it, Shreve. That hurts."

"Oh, I'm sorry, your Royal Highness." Shreve feigned another punch at Cates. Cates covered up laughing. Across the street, burly Art Vasquez came out of Valley Hardware with a broom and started sweeping the sidewalk in front of the store.

"Hey, *Ese*," Frank called over to Art using the Spanish article all the Boll Weevil athletes used to refer to their Mexican teammates. Art waved his broom.

"*Ese*, you're a senior now. You better kick Holtville's tail this fall."

"You got it, Shreve. But it'll be tough without you guys. We're going to miss you, Shreve. You, too, Frank."

"Aw, you guys'll be great. You can do it."

"That's right." Shreve agreed.

"Look." Cates tapped Frank on the leg. "There's a semi coming. Let's go watch him knock some bricks off the hotel."

"Okay." Frank hopped off the wall. Shreve jumped down, too, echoing Frank's okay. "Jinx, you owe me a Coke."

"Screw you."

"See you guys." Art turned to go back into the hardware store.

"See you, Art." Frank headed on down the sidewalk toward the corner.

Shreve and Cates waved to Art and quickly caught up with Frank in front of the post office. Shreve faked a shoulder block at Frank then punched Cates again.

"Oww, Shreve. That hurts, you big ugly son-of-a-buck."

Cates swung half-heartedly at Shreve, but Shreve dodged. Cates broke into a run for the intersection. Shreve and Frank took off after him.

2

IT WAS SUMMER IN COTTON and as usual, already getting hot. Damn blue uniforms, Lar complained to himself, if Bob Lowell wasn't such a cheapskate we wouldn't start sweating like pigs until maybe noon instead of ten. Lowell's so damn tight even the stingy-ass farmers will probably get rid of hizzoner this fall. Wouldn't be the worse thing for Cotton, either.

Lar often wondered how he'd gotten to Cotton, a little half-horse town in the hottest part of the Imperial Valley where the most exciting thing to do was watch all the crops grow and all the Mexicans—Lar called them "Mesicans"—harvest them. It wasn't that Enid, Oklahoma, had been any great shakes, nor the Army neither, but somehow he'd drifted out here to California and, with his experience as an MP in Korea, finally landed a police job after drifting through a half dozen or so mostly farmhand jobs around Cotton.

Lar was a natural for the job, bringing with him a strong sense of where people belonged and in what place. He did a bang-up job keeping migrant bracero workers, poor local Mexicans, blacks, and whites who lived beyond the grain elevators east of the railroad tracks away from Cotton's small, but growing and mostly white middle class population.

He was appropriately obsequious to the wealthy farmers of Cotton, especially the Cotton family itself, and was as good about turning the other way when the good kids got rowdy as he was about pursuing his duty when the ones who weren't supposed to step out of line did so.

He had a reputation all over town for being tough, and there were many who lived in the shadow of the grain vaults who could personally attest to that. The other kids, like Frank Mason, Shreve West, and Jimmy Cates, whom Lar watched crossing the road as they made their way toward him, looked up to Lar and thought of him as the friendly, local cop. He was sort of an unofficial big brother to them, though they treated him rather more deferentially and with more of a sense of intimidation than most older brothers would inspire. They had heard the stories about Lar and thought they might be true.

"What'd'ya say, boys?" Frank and his friends crowded around the police car.

Lar had noticed Carol Scott and Marcie Cotton Clayborn walking up the sidewalk across the street and hated to take his eyes off either of them, especially Carol. Lar thought she might be a little sweet on him.

"Hey, Lar." Jimmy greeted he cop. "What's up?"

"The sky, I reckon."

The boys laughed, like they thought Lar was grown-up and witty. Lar looked for Carol and Marcie but they had apparently ducked into a store out of the sun.

"Hot enough for you?" Shreve asked.

"Shit, it ain't even started yet. You boys ought to know that better than me. You still working with them Mesican *braceros*?"

"We all got better jobs already." Frank said.

"A couple of weeks is long enough out there doing slave work, huh?"

"I reckon it is."

"Did you hear that Richard Nixon was coming to Cotton, Lar?"

Frank snickered. Shreve shrugged his shoulders, grunted, and looked up at the hazy summer sky.

"No, can't say as I did."

"Oh, yeah." Cates explained his latest rumor. "He's going to drive down from Palm Springs real soon."

"Jeez," Shreve grunted.

"Did you know that, Lar?" Jimmy repeated.

"I expect," Lar killed the Nixon trip with the simple fact of his official insight, "that if old Dick Nixon was coming to Cotton, somebody would've let Mayor Lowell know so he could put on more officers and that means he would've let me know and he ain't, so I doubt that Nixon's coming, do you, boy?"

"Well. . ." Cates stammered. "Well, it could have happened."

Frank hadn't joined in the latest round of teasing because he was looking back down the road where it came in from the south. The wail of a siren was beginning to build and he could see the familiar markings on a fast moving car roaring into Cotton. It was a big California Highway Patrol Chrysler cruiser and it was fairly flying.

3

AHH." TEDDY MARTINEZ SIGHED AS he entered Dale Honeycutt's barber shop. "You got the air conditioner fixed. Feels great."

"Did it just so's you could come in here and sit on your scrawny Mexican ass." Dale growled. Teddy laughed.

He and Dale went all the way back to Korea together. They were the only two of Cotton's nine boys who went to Korea who came back. Dale returned on a hospital ship. He had been shot out of his sniper's tree and left for dead. The bullet scars on his arms, cheek, and chest—for those who knew about the ones hidden by his work clothes—attested to the closeness with which he nearly became the eighth Cotton boy not to return. Locals sometimes complained of Cotton's disproportionate loss and sacrifice. Dale never did. He was a fatalist.

"Shut the damn door or I'll put the swamp cooler back in here so you'll feel more at home."

"Oh, a swamp cooler is a Mexican air conditioner now, is it?" Teddy shut the door and took a seat in front of Dale, who lounged in one of his two new barber chairs.

"That's right." A crooked grin creased the scar on Dale's cheek.

"You better tell some of your white brethren about that, then. There's still more swamp coolers in the valley than air conditioners."

"Heathens. The modern predicament."

"Oh, no, not that again. I suppose it's going to be my fault again."

"Why, yes, by God, it is partly your fault."

"You're not gonna start up about me managing All-American again are you?"

"Why the hell not? That's what you're doing, ain't it?"

"You know I am."

"So you're driving Manny Ruiz out of business," Dale argued.

Outside, he saw Reverend Wilcox, the new minister over in black town, pass by in the company of a sober-looking black girl.

"I am not," Teddy denied.

"The hell you ain't. Manny's been trying to make a go of it for ten years and just when he's going good, you open up All-American and Manny's starts going downhill."

"Boy, you're on a rampage today. I just walked in the door and I'm destroying Cotton already."

"Well, you're a hometown boy and on the city council. You're supposed to help Cotton, not wreck it. Bob Lowell's good enough at that, thank you."

"That's why I came by, Dale."

"You mean no haircut?"

"Seriously, what do you think about me running for mayor?"

"I'd think you're crazy."

"Come on. I'm being straight."

"Well . . . oh, my, look at that."

"What, what? Damn it, Dale."

But Teddy followed Dale's line of sight to the shop's big front window. Two women were walking by outside and had stopped for a moment. One was a young girl, blonde, thin, and attractive. The other was a brunette, a lady in her early thirties, shorter than the girl and especially nice-looking.

"Lord almighty, Marcie Clayborn gets better looking every year, don't she?"

"A real grown woman." Teddy agreed, "but a hell of a one to hold onto."

"Old Jeff can't do it, can he?"

"Apparently not, from all the stories anyway. The other one's Billy Cotton's girl, ain't it?"

"Nice little filly, too. Since Billy left I think she and Lar got something going."

"Well, she's a good looking girl, too. They don't stay alone for long."

"But she ain't a Marcie."

"Not many are." The women moved down the sidewalk and out of sight. "But she's damn good enough for government work."

"Lordy, lordy. I believe Marcie would be worth the wrath of Jeff Clayborn and her old daddy King, too, huh?"

"I wouldn't want to cross King Cotton on no account."

"Especially if you're going to be his mayor, eh?"

"You're becoming a grouchy old man."

"When I came to on that cold Korean ground I was a grouchy old man."

"I don't doubt it."

For a few moments, the two men stared out Dale's big window. They saw old Homer Cole, the town bum, go by picking around garbage cans. Then a couple of lost-looking *braceros* straggled by—and some local boys who crossed the street to talk to Lar Turner, parked as usual at the filling station by the main intersection.

"Cotton is changing. For the worse."

"Oh, I don't know, maybe it's not all bad."

"Looky there." Dale jumped out of his chair. "Here comes a highway patrol car and he's barreling through town."

They went to the window and watched the CHP cruiser blast through the four-way without stopping, sparks flying from underneath where the frame scraped the concrete of the road. Seconds later, they saw the boys scatter and Lar jerk the squad car onto the highway and take off after the CHP. They could hear his tires squealing above the hum of the air conditioner.

"Damn Lar," Dale remarked, "there he goes chasing after the highway patrol like it was any of his business. Thinking he's a big shot. His kind is what's ruining Cotton."

"His kind is what Cotton is. The only difference between him and King Cotton is the money they take home every month."

Dale gave Teddy a long, questioning look. But he didn't say anything.

4

KATE MASON WAS FILING INVOICES when Reverend Wilcox and Sandra Glover came into York's Electric.

"Why, hello, Reverend Wilcox, Sandra." Kate looked up from her work. "How are you all today?"

"Just fine, thank you, Mrs. Mason." Even though he had lived down the hall from the Masons for several months, the reverend always spoke formally to both of them. "And good day to you."

"Hi, Mrs. Mason." Sandra stood to one side of the reverend in front of the counter. There was a short, slightly uncomfortable pause. Kate broke into it.

"So, what is it that I can do for you?"

The reverend took a clean, white handkerchief from a dark suit pocket and mopped his sweating brow. He wore a dark suit every day, whether it was sixty degrees outside or one hundred and twenty. Yawning, Sandra looked out at the sidewalk just as Marcie Clayborn and Carol Scott passed by chatting animatedly.

"Well, now." The reverend had a fine bass voice. "It seems that my flock is being plagued by an errant record player."

"An errant record player?"

"Yes, ma'am. It's a devilish machine. Sometimes it works and sometimes it don't. We use it to back up our choir, you know, pianos being so expensive these days."

"Oh, I'm sure."

"Would it be possible to trouble Mr. York to take a look at our machine? We'll be happy to pay for his services with cash money."

"Why, of course." Kate picked up a pad of forms and a pen. "You just leave it here and I'll make out a work order on it. Mr. York will get to it as soon as he can. In a day or two, I suspect. All right?"

"That'll be fine. We'll do with just the choir tomorrow, but it would be nice to have it back by the next Sabbath."

"I'm sure it'll be ready by Monday or Tuesday."

"Nice, very nice."

"You have it outside, or where is it?" Kate peered past Reverend Wilcox. He looked down at his well-polished shoes for a moment then back at Kate.

"I don't have it with me just now. I'll have one of the young brothers from my flock drop it by later if that will be all right."

"Of course." Kate set down the pad of forms. "We'll be open until five-thirty."

"Then I'll see to it that it's here by then."

"There's Frank, Mrs. Mason." Sandra pointed outside the store. Kate squinted at the bright street outside.

"Is he with somebody?"

"Looks like Shreve West and Jimmy Cates."

"Talking to Lar Turner, no doubt."

"Yes, ma'am." Sandra frowned at the sound of Lar's name. Kate noticed.

"The boys get bored when they aren't working. I guess Lar is interesting because he's the law." Sandra was silent and looked away from Kate, who changed the subject. "I think it's nice that you and Frank and some of the other kids from your class will be going to Valley this fall, Sandra. That should be. . ."

"Uh-oh." Reverend Wilcox interrupted. "Something's happening out there. Here comes the highway patrol." Sandra and Kate quickly joined him at the front window.

"Sure enough. Why he's going pall mall through town."

"Heaven's sakes," the reverend exclaimed.

They watched Frank and his friends quickly back away from the Cotton squad car as Lar jammed it into gear and blasted out into the street in pursuit of the CHP cruiser.

"Well, I'll be. Will you look at that Turner boy taking off like that in the police car? Why, he's a veritable abomination upon lawbreakers, isn't he?" Kate nodded.

"He's an abomination, all right." Sandra began a little louder and a little more emotionally than perhaps she had intended. "But not upon. . . ."

She stopped herself and turned back toward the interior of the store. Kate and the reverend looked over in surprise, then at one another. Sandra busied herself with an appraisal of a nearby on-sale vacuum cleaner. In the quiet of the store, they heard the tires on Lar's squad car squealing as he raced out of town.

5

WITH SHREVE ADROITLY MAKING THE last corner before the highway opened up for eight straight miles to Northland, Frank remembered the last such high speed run he'd made with Shreve and Cates—their graduation night in early summer.

Bolstered by a few illegal beers, they'd accepted Donnie Hodges' challenge of a race to Brawley. Shreve rode shotgun in Cates' souped-up Mercury, with Frank in the back seat. Right at midnight, they lined up side-by-side with Donnie and his buddy Gilbert Cruz out on the highway heading south. They taunted Cates over the roar of the revving engines.

"That piece of crap won't do sixty," Cruz yelled.

"Screw you." Shreve called back across Cates. Cruz flipped him off.

A second later they sped down the highway, Cates a little ahead. They rushed away from Cotton, past crop fields and the smelly stockyard, pushing eighty, then ninety, then from out of nowhere headlights from another vehicle came straight at them.

"Shit." Cates hit the steering wheel with an open palm. "Shit."

He backed the Mercury down. Donnie and Gilbert happily sailed past, shifting back into the right lane just in time to miss the oncoming car. Frank was the first to realize who they'd passed.

"Oh, hell, Jimmy," he yelped, seeing the familiar black and white Chrysler shoot by, "it's the CHP."

While Cates drove his foot hard into the gas pedal, Frank turned to watch the big police car brake violently and spin around in the road behind them, lights flashing crazily. Ahead, Donnie and Gilbert were long gone.

Shouting for Cates to hurry up, they kept a keen eye peeled for the CHP as they dropped into and out of a couple of small, bridged creek beds. Finally, Cates spotted a county road heading west.

"Hold on. I'm taking this road."

He made the ninety-degree turn at more than forty, rocks and dust flying as they spun into the gravel and dirt alongside the road. Somehow he got the Merc back on the pavement and immediately cut the lights, flooring the gas again.

They rolled the windows down and navigated by the white lines along the edge of the pavement for two or three heart-stopping miles before they were sure they'd lost the CHP. With a cheer they slapped each other on the shoulders. Cates turned the lights back on and when they found a road running off to the left they turned onto it, taking the chance to go on into Brawley for a late-night hamburger and root beer.

Cates' banging on the cab of the pickup brought Frank out of his memory-induced reverie of graduation night. A bad idea occurred to him.

"What if this is the same CHP we outran on graduation night?"

"Ah." Shreve dismissed the idea. "No way. We were in Cates' car and it was night. He never saw us, man."

"I hope not."

Cates banged on the cab again and when Frank turned around, Cates pressed his face against the cab window, distorting his mouth and nose into a twisted mass of flesh.

"Idiot." Shreve looked in the rearview mirror.

Frank made a face at Cates. Cates leaned over by Frank's window.

"Ruf, ruf," he barked. "Arf, arf."

6

THERE IT IS, SHREVE." FRANK pointed up ahead.

The police car lights flashed and wavered, floating in the watery, hot-air mirage rising above the baking asphalt road. Cotton field after cotton field stretched off in the distance. The Chocolate Mountains rose reddish-brown from the desert floor. They and the dirt road that led to them were as plain in the clear desert air as if they were within arm's length instead of twenty-five miles past Northland.

"Must be big." Shreve eased off the gas.

"Cates, can you see what happened up there?" Frank called out the window.

"Looks like a semi and something else from here." Cates stood in the pickup bed. "Yeah, a semi and a car."

"Looks bad."

Lar Turner was in the middle of the road directing traffic around the semi, which angled across both lanes. Shreve brought the pickup to a stop behind a sedan while a couple of pickups and a produce truck, their drivers gawking, took to the shoulder to get by. There were a couple of cars to the right of the road behind the CHP cruiser and Lar's vehicle.

From where they were now, Frank could see the wrecked car. It was off the road to the right and had spun around facing back toward the highway. The bumper dangled on one side and the hood was completely smashed, steam still rising from the caved-in radiator. The front windshield was gone except for shards along the side. It was totaled. The truck, on the other hand, had surprisingly little damage to it. A smashed fender and punched in grill, but not much else to show for a full-speed crash.

In front of the truck, the highway cop and a couple of other people bent down tending to someone lying in the sandy dirt beside the road. Another man, apparently the truck driver, walked back and forth in front of the CHP officer. The man kept clasping his head with his hands, over and over.

"Whew." Shreve blew out a breath. "A head-on. Man, it was head-on."

"Yeah," Frank mumbled. He couldn't see the man by the road yet, but he could hear him. The man was groaning and crying.

"It's old Harold Wade." Cates was right by Frank's ear, causing him to jump involuntarily. "Ah, man, he's really hurt. Listen to him."

"Harold Wade. Bound to have been drunk then. I ain't never seen him when he wasn't drunk or drinking. Can you see, Frank? Is he real bad? He ought to be dead after a wreck like that."

Frank didn't answer. Everything seemed to move in a kind of slow motion. Mostly all he heard now was Harold Wade groaning and cursing. It was hard to imagine anyone could dream up the epithets the writhing man unleashed at the CHP officer, the truck driver, the air, an obviously uncaring and malevolent God.

Shreve eased the pickup closer to where Harold lay jerking around beside the road. The CHP and the drivers of the parked cars were trying to keep Harold from hurting himself any worse.

"Help me hold him." The CHP officer directed two men standing to one side. "He's gonna tear himself up." Behind the CHP vehicle, the truck driver kept pacing back and forth. He seemed to be in shock.

Up closer, Frank could see that Harold was hurt bad. His arms were scraped raw and bloody, one leg was bleeding and twisted—obviously broken—and his hair was matted with blood from an unseen wound. Frank gaped at the injured, raging man. He barely heard Lar and Shreve talking.

"You boys move on." Lar seemed to be trying to impress the highway patrolman. "Let's clear the area for emergency work here. Let's go."

"How bad is he?" Shreve raised an eyebrow at the local cop.

"He ran right into that truck. Serves him right."

"He's just an old drunk. Ain't nobody deserve to get smashed up like that, just 'cause he's a sot."

"Okay, let's move it." Lar used his best drill sergeant voice. "You boys get the hell out of here. You're blocking a police investigation."

Shreve jabbed the pickup in gear and whipped it around the semi. Cates had to grab the frame around Frank's open window to keep from falling out. Frank kept looking back at the wreck as they headed up the highway toward Northland. Shreve was really pissed at Lar.

"Go to hell. Asshole."

"What are you mad at Lar for?"

"I don't know, I just never seen him act like that before, that's all. He acted like he was some kind of big shot. Like he never seen us before or something."

"Oh."

No one spoke again until Shreve took the next unpaved left and headed west toward the Salton Sea.

"We'll go back to Cotton the back way. Come in out by Desert Cotton Gin and go by school into town. Maybe somebody will be out and about by then."

"Okay," Frank agreed easily, "whatever you think. It's your pickup."

Out of the corner of his eye, Frank saw Shreve glance over at him. In back, Cates had found a seat on an old tire in the bed of the pickup and was quiet for a change. Shreve put his foot hard into the gas pedal and steered the truck down the bumpy dirt road. Behind the speeding pickup, dust rose in a swirling cloud that floated above the cotton fields, to slowly settle back down as a light brown covering on the maturing green plants.

7

F RANK PILED STACKS OF WASHERS on cotton picker spindle arms in Buck Clayborn's tin shed while Vince Scully and Jerry Doggett called an afternoon Dodgers game on the radio. Frank labored monotonously in the 110 degree plus heat, mentally playing back the hardest line drive he'd hit last spring for Cotton High.

Buck himself was trying to get a "*Wear Cotton Es Mucho Culo*" sticker—a match for one on the bumper of his big, dusty pickup—to stay on the wavy sheet metal wall in the shed. All the while he complained to his other worker, chunky, amiable Juan Cota, about the lack of good cotton picker drivers in the valley.

Juan understood maybe every fourth word Buck said, but he smiled and nodded while sweat streamed down his dark brown face.

"Damn lazy bastards." Buck summed up the local farm work force. "None of them want to work—they just want to get paid."

"*Sí.*" Juan agreed, showing a big, white-toothed grin.

"They come out here," Buck ignored Juan's pleasantness, "looking for a handout. Things go bad back in Texas or Oklahoma, or wherever the hell it is they all come from, and they come out here looking for paradise or some damn thing or the other. It sure ain't work they're looking for."

"*Sí, jefe.*" Juan agreed again, wiping a thick black lock off his forehead with a hand oily from the hundreds and hundreds of washers he'd slid onto spindles since the work day began, as always, promptly at six a.m.

"The whole damn country's getting this way. Everybody bellowing about what's owed to them, but nobody wanting to do their part. Nothing but taking, no giving, no responsibility. That's the word—responsibility. *Comprende,* Pancho Villa?"

"*Sí, patron.*" Juan did not understand. "*Comprendo. Yo entiendo.*"

"Good. Oh, hell, you don't get a damn thing. You Mesicans are..." Buck began again, then stopped. He noticed Frank was not loading washers very quickly. After a minute or so, he cleared his throat loudly and addressed his young worker. "Ain't that right, Mason?"

Frank didn't realize Buck was talking to him right away, because in his mind he was hook sliding safely into second base beneath the tag of Rancho Verde's quick little shortstop. Right hand resting motionless atop a spindle, he unconsciously moved his body as the hook slide came to a successful conclusion.

"Hey," Buck yelled, "what in hell are you doing, dreaming? Wake up, boy."

"What, what." Frank dropped a spindle full of washers all over the shed floor. Buck and Juan laughed while Frank hurried to retrieve the washers.

"I didn't hear you." Frank got back to his feet and put together another string of washers to slide onto the spindle.

"I said, 'ain't that right?'" Buck repeated. "I was just telling General Santy Anny here that this country's going to hell faster'n you can say Jack Robinson."

"I reckon things are different nowadays," Frank allowed.

"You bet your ass they are." Buck jumped back onto the current bandwagon of many no-longer-young residents of Cotton. "You got lazy bastards everywhere you turn, uppity coons going to white schools, and there's more wetbacks in the valley than there are white people."

Frank glanced over at Juan but he didn't seem to have understood.

"I don't know, Mr. Clayborn. It seems complicated to me."

"Complicated? What the hell's complicated about it?"

"Well, it seems like things are changing in a real big way."

Frank thought about the big demonstrations back east he'd read about in the papers, about the stories of fighting in Indochina, about predictions of changes sweeping the U.S. and the world. It all seemed vast, unfathomable, and scary.

"I'm not sure if I want to live through all what's getting ready to happen."

"What?" Buck exploded. "What kind of crap are you talking, boy? What a load of bull that is. Don't want to live through it? What are you going to do, throw yourself under a tractor?"

"I meant—"

"Hell, boy, you're the kind of stupid lunkhead that's gonna let the coons walk all over us and let 'em take everything. Soon it'll be their damn country. There won't be no place for a white man. Shee-it."

Frank looked over at Juan, who smiled back, a lost look on his face. Juan didn't know the language. Buck did, but hadn't understood him, either.

Frank wanted to say that he felt so small, so insignificant, so unsure of himself in the face of what seemed to be on the horizon for American society that he wasn't sure what to do, or when to do it, or how. He was just a kid and he didn't understand what was happening. But he hadn't said that. He couldn't. He didn't know how.

8

AFTER LUNCH, RAIN DELAYED THE Dodgers game in Chicago and the local station went back to its regular programming. As the only radio station in the north end of the valley, KCOT—called KCLOT or KSNOT by Cotton's young people—played a mixture of country and rock music that reflected the age and interest range of their listeners.

Willie Nelson's high twang on "Half a Man" or a Lefty Frizzell song or perhaps the latest from Johnny Tillotson filled in the gaps between the sounds of washers sliding onto spindle arms and the occasional exchange between Frank and Juan, with Juan mostly smiling knowingly and repeating "*El jefe es loco,*" as Buck banged around the shed between trips out to one of his fields.

Buck had just come back from one of these trips and groused around the shed throwing tools this way and that when a big, new, white Olds 88 with dark-tinted windows pulled alongside the shed in a cloud of dust.

"*Quién es?*" The two workers joined Buck in staring at the large vehicle.

"*No sé.* I don't know. Maybe it's Mrs. Clayborn?"

"Boss wife?"

"No, no boss wife." Buck growled at his two employees. "Boss's brother's wife."

"Oh, *sí.*"

The driver's door opened and out stepped Marcie Cotton Clayborn, Buck's sister-in-law. She looked impossibly cool and beautiful in an off-white muslin dress.

"*Ay, Chihuahua.*" Juan whistled under his breath.

Frank missed the end of the spindle arm in his hand and sent another collection of washers rattling across the shed floor. He expected another chewing out, but Buck turned back to his tools like nobody had just driven up and Frank hadn't screwed up again.

On hands and knees retrieving washers, Frank looked up to see Billy Cotton's girl, Carol Scott, climb out of the passenger side and join Marcie. Carol looked like a younger, not quite so impressive, lighter-haired and lighter-skinned version of Marcie. Either woman was enough to rattle Frank, but both together left him feeling like a sub-literate dullard with speech and hearing problems.

"Afternoon, brother-in-law, dear." Marcie addressed Buck, then, "Hi, boys," to Frank and Juan.

"*Buenas tardes, señora.*"

"Hello, ma'am." Frank stood. His mouth felt as dry as the desert ground outside the shed.

"Hi, Frank."

"Hi, Carol."

"Well, well, well." Buck dramatically turned to face the women. "What do we have here? I do believe it's my dazzling sister-in-law, the Princess of Cotton, the queen of air conditioning. I hear tell a person can get frostbite from riding in that refrigerated boat of yours."

"Only from May fifteenth to September fifteenth, you handsome devil, you. You know that."

"So, tell me, Princess Queenie, to what do I owe the honor of your majesty's visit? Even got you a lady-in-waiting today, huh?"

Carol Scott rocked on her heels, clearly uncomfortable under Buck's steady gaze.

"Now, you know, Buck, that tonight's the barbecue and Jeff sent me out here to get that big cooler of yours."

"Sounds like him—send you around on errands. I don't believe my little brother's all there sometimes."

"You always were the handsomest and the smartest."

"Then how come, by damn, I'm out here in this god-awful hot shed with a Mex who don't understand a word I say and a boy who's afraid of his own shadow instead of gallivanting around in an air-conditioned car with a fine woman like you?"

"Just luck, I guess." Marcie winked at Frank, who nearly dropped another stack of washers.

"If I didn't have bad luck," Buck pretended to complain, heading over to his truck to get the cooler, "I wouldn't have no luck at all."

"How are you boys doing?" Marcie walked over to Frank and Juan. Juan nodded several times. Carol followed. "How's your momma, Frank?"

"She's doing just fine, Mrs. Clayborn. She works at York's now, ma'am."

"Yes, I know."

"Still does some weekends and holidays up at Galvan's in Northland."

"Your mother's a hard worker. A strong woman."

"Yes, ma'am."

"Stop calling me, ma'am," Marcie chided. "I ain't your grandma. You can take this southern gentleman stuff too far, you know?"

"Yes, ma'am, uh, Mrs. Clayborn."

"Marcie. Call me Marcie."

"Okay." Frank looked down at the ground.

Buck slammed the trunk of the Olds and headed back into the shed. Marcie started to leave, then stopped and spoke to Frank in a lowered voice.

"Be sure to say hello to your friend Shreve for me, will you?" Frank looked at her a little surprised.

"Okay."

"Be sure you do." She gave him one of her stunning smiles. "Promise?"

"Promise... Marcie."

Marcie winked at him again and headed for her car.

"Bye, Frank." Carol followed after Marcie.

"Bye, Carol." Frank looked over at Juan and got a big shit-eating grin in return. "See you around."

"You boys get back to work." Buck stomped back into the shed. "You *entiendo* me?"

"Yes, sir." Frank was happier for the moment than he figured Buck liked to see any of his workers.

"*Sí, sí, patron.*" Juan piled up another load of washers.

"Jesus," Buck swore. "What a pair of jackasses I gotta work with."

9

I DON'T UNDERSTAND HOW YOU ACT like you do around men when you're already married." Carol and Marcie drove to Manny Ruiz's to get Buck's cooler filled with ice. "I could never do that to Billy."

"Oh, please, honey." Marcie rolled her eyes. "Cool it with the saintly routine, will you?"

"As long as Billy and me are going together," Carol vowed, "I couldn't look at another guy, much less flirt with one."

"Give me a break." Marcie waved at Frank Mason's uncle, Carl Waters, who drove by in his red Jeep. He gave Marcie a happy, toothless grin. Marcie stopped at the intersection by the city park then headed on toward Main Street.

"You know, Carol, you don't have to play the Blessed Virgin with me just because I'm Billy's big sister. Shoot, honey, as far as I'm concerned when Billy joined the army that ended your responsibility to him."

"Not for me."

"Carol, I got eyes."

"What do you mean?"

"I mean you and Lar."

"Me and Lar?"

"Listen to me, Carol." Marcie pulled up to the stop sign at Main Street.

"You know me. I believe a girl should do what she feels like and with who she feels like doing it with. And it's nobody's business. Even in a town like Cotton where everything is everybody else's business, especially boy-girl stuff."

"But we're not doing anything," Carol insisted. "Besides, if I were looking for a boy, which I'm not, it would be somebody like Shreve West, not an older man like Lar Turner."

Carol watched for a reaction at the mention of Shreve's name. Marcie acted like she hadn't heard a thing. She made a smooth right turn and headed down Main toward Cotton's little strip of a downtown. A couple of firemen at the station across the street waved at Marcie but she didn't seem to see them.

"Don't you care about Jeff at all?"

"Jeff and I reached an agreement some time ago. He gets to be King Cotton's son-in-law and business partner, I get to do what I want."

"Even have other men?"

"Yes."

"Shreve West?"

"If we found each other appealing."

Carol sat back in her seat and said nothing else. Marcie made a U-turn in the middle of the street at the four-way stop and pulled up to the curb outside Manny's market. She looked over at Carol and gave her a big-sisterly smile.

"Look, hon, you don't have to act like me, or approve of the way I live. All of us are different, and that's okay with me. Real okay. But I do want you to listen to me on this one thing. Don't let Lar sweet talk you into doing something you don't want to. He's no good."

"Him no good? How can you say something like that? You of all people."

The air inside the car seemed to get cooler yet and it was Marcie's turn to sigh. Carol looked over, eyes welling up.

"I'm sorry, Marcie, I didn't mean to say such a mean thing."

"Don't worry about it, I should've never butted in. I just don't like seeing young girls taken advantage of."

"I can take care of myself. I'm a woman now, not a kid like I used to be."

Marcie opened her door and slid a finely shaped leg out onto the street. In an instant, a blast of desert summer heat wiped out the cool air in the Olds.

"Sure you are, hon. Sure you are."

10

RICHARD MARTIN LOADED A PAPER plate with his second hamburger and a huge handful of potato chips and then sat back down by Mrs. Mason who was perched on a big ironwood log.

The sun, so yellow and hot during the middle of the day, had lost its power and bathed the desert floor in a mild, tranquil gold.

"Aunt Jean," Frank moved over to the campfire where his mother's older sister cooked up several more burgers, "can I have another one of those?"

"Sure you can." Aunt Jean loaded a smoking meat patty onto a hamburger bun generously spread with mayonnaise and mustard and eased it beside the pile of potato chips on his plate.

Tired from a full day bouncing about in the Jeep, climbing on rocks, and hiking up washes like the one in which they had camped for the evening, Frank breathed in the cool peacefulness of the open desert.

The dried, salty sweat that coated his body after an outing like this made him feel as fully alive as he thought possible. Being outside in the sun, the wind, and the sand was real, and it made him feel real at a time when he often felt little in his life actually was. He inhaled the odor of the land and the food, and with it a sense of joy—to be alive, to be with his family and his buddy Richard.

"This is the life, isn't it?" Richard called out, expressing Frank's thoughts.

Frank moved over to a flat rock near his Uncle Carl, who sat sideways in the front seat of his Jeep, his feet hanging outside.

"You bet." Frank took a big bite of his sandwich.

He picked up a half-empty bottle of Coke and took a long swig. The soda was beginning to warm up, but was still cool enough to be satisfying.

"This is a great spread, Mrs. Waters." Richard made a precise high sign with his thumb and index finger. "Top notch."

"Better watch that food, boy." Carl teased the fastidious Cotton High salutatorian. "Careful you don't mix mustard up with your dress slacks there."

"Oh, no, Mr. Waters. Can't do that, these are my finest. I usually wear these jeans to church. Sort of my Sunday-go-to-meetings, you know." Richard extracted a comb and pretended to run it through his hair. "Mustn't allow ourselves to be messed up by the natural elements."

"You silly galoot." Kate shook her head.

"Madame." Richard adopted a mock formal tone. "I am thoroughly wounded by this scurrilous, familial attack against my personal grooming habits."

"Heaven's sake." Aunt Jean shook her head as she fixed another burger. "You sound like a talking dictionary."

"Please." Richard proclaimed. "I am a veritable fountain of information. I am full of words and knowledge."

"You're full of something all right." Kate shook her head.

"Oh." Richard groaned, grabbing his chest. "Straight through the heart. I beg of you, madame, clemency, clemency."

Everyone laughed, especially Carl. In the late afternoon sun, a ray of light streaked across his face, glistening on a small glob of mustard and mayonnaise in the corner of his mouth. Frank admired his uncle's completely unabashed lack of self-consciousness and that little bit of sauce reminded him of his first day in the valley just over two years before.

Two things surprised Frank when he first stepped off the Trailways bus in El Centro. A blast of hot, desert air—and his Uncle Carl.

Dressed in faded dungarees, a long sleeve work shirt, dusty, well-worn leather boots and a sweat-stained straw hat, Carl looked every bit the transplanted Okie. His brand new Jeep made it clear he dressed the way he did out of choice, not necessity.

"I reckon you must be Frank."

"Yes, sir. Uncle Carl?"

"Sure enough, son." Carl smiled broadly, showing two bright pink gums and no teeth. Frank smiled back, amazed that Carl seemed to be unaware, or at least unconcerned, that he had no teeth in his head.

"Well, if you're ready, we might as well head on back home. The old woman and your momma'll be waiting on us."

"Okay."

They hadn't talked much on the way to Cotton. The valley, in all its newness and differentness, bombarded Frank's senses. The constant hot wind on his face, the scrub desert surrounding huge cultivated fields with green plants Frank didn't recognize.

They passed by the dusty little towns with already browning lawns, and the long, flat earth stretched out as far as one could see—broken from time to time by patches of tamarack and oleander trees and by occasional rows of neatly trimmed palms.

Frank didn't see much of Cotton that first day, what with the reunion with his mother and seeing Aunt Jean for the first time since he was a little kid. She made a big batch of hamburgers and for the first time he had the mixture of mayonnaise and mustard sauce he always associated with his genial aunt and uncle.

"Well, Frank, how was your bus ride?"

"It was just fine, Aunt Jean. But, gosh, I had a present for you then it got stolen in El Paso."

"Oh, no. That's terrible. You didn't lose your money, too, did you?"

"Huh-uh, Mom." Frank blushed. "I still got it in my shoe like you had me do."

"Goodness." Aunt Jean teased. "You better get it out of there or it'll take to stinking so bad nobody'll change it."

The adults shared a laugh that Frank didn't join in on. He set his burger and Coke down and dug the twenty-dollar bill out of his right shoe where it had traveled from the Ozark Mountains to the Imperial Valley nestled safely between sock and insole.

"You want it back, Mom?"

"Lord, no. Not after where it's been for God knows how long."

Uncle Carl let out a good-sized cackle then, his gums exposed in all their healthy pinkness, another little blob of sauce lodged in the corner of his mouth.

A rumbling sound brought Frank out of those first Cotton memories to see a Jeep round a canyon wall up the wash from the camp. The vehicle sped by the campsite, a cloud of dust in its wake. The driver waved and called out "*¿Qué pasa?*"

"*Nada.*" Frank answered without thinking, returning the wave to the surprised driver who looked back as the Jeep barreled on down the wash. Aunt Jean gave Frank an admiring smile.

"I'm sure glad you were here to answer that smart-alecky guy in the Jeep. Him roaring past here like such a big shot and all. I guess you told him."

"Shoot." Frank lowered his head, looking shy but proud like a farm boy who'd just won a blue ribbon at the county fair. "It wasn't nothing, Aunt Jean, heck."

11

Y OU KNOW, RICHARD," FRANK STIRRED the dying campfire with a small stick, "I've lived here a couple of years now and I ain't never seen Billy Cotton. Sometimes I don't think he's a real person."

"He's real all right." It was completely dark now and the boys' figures were barely discernible in the flickering light. "He's the biggest deal ever came out of Cotton."

"Really good jock, huh?"

"The greatest."

"Better'n Shreve?"

"Yeah."

"Whew, that's saying something."

"It sure is."

"It's funny I've never seen him."

"Hmm, just luck, I guess, or bad luck. Depends on how you look at it. He left before you got here."

"Is he a good guy, too?"

"Sure, Shreve's probably got him a little there."

"Boy, that Shreve. If I was as big and good as he was I'd go to San Diego State or Arkansas even, somewhere to play ball instead of at Valley."

"I heard he might not even go there."

"Sometimes he talks like that, but he keeps stuff to himself mostly."

"Guys like Billy Cotton and Shreve are different than us."

"Yeah. You know, I played on all the teams and did okay but, hey, all the girls love Shreve. He could have anyone he wanted."

"He's big and strong and good looking. He's cool. Girls like him."

"Damn Shreve."

"He got all the luck, didn't he." Richard stretched his legs out by the fire.

"Sure did."

"You know, I'm stiff as a board from riding in the Jeep all day."

"Fairly cramped quarters, wasn't it?"

"Yeah, and my feet were up on the big cooler, too."

The fire was almost dead and the stars were out, bright and infinite in the clear desert sky. The boys were quiet for several moments and the evening continued to blanket the desert with its still darkness.

"There it is," Richard broke into the lull, "like you say."

"What?"

"The noise of silence."

"The *roar* of silence," Frank corrected. "It's quiet now, for sure, but it's better in the afternoon, when it's real still and hot. That's when you hear it best. Like a wind blowing inside your head."

"Oh."

"So, Richard," Frank shifted the conversation, "are you mad you didn't get valedictorian?"

"How did you get from the roar of silence to valedictorian?"

"Just thinking, that's all. You should've got it."

"You should've been athlete-scholar, too."

"I don't know."

"Well, I'm satisfied with salutatorian. We did well at old CHS."

"I suppose."

"Sure, we had a great time."

"What do you want to be now?"

"I don't know, first I go to Oregon State, then be a mathematician, maybe an engineer. How about you?"

"Geez." Frank's melancholy voice carried softly in the dark. "I don't know. I used to want to be a ball player. Now I'm not sure. There's VJC. At least I know Cates is going, too. After that—maybe the service."

"The service?"

"Yeah, I guess. Buck Clayborn says things are heating up over in, uh. . . ."

"Indochina."

"That's it."

"I wouldn't base my life on Buck Clayborn's opinions."

"I didn't mean that exactly. I just meant that if there was a war."

"Ah, I doubt there'll be a war. You'll have to think of something else."

"Well, we don't have to decide tonight, do we?"

"Shoot, no. We're young. We have our whole lives ahead of us."

"You bet we do. It's all ahead of us. We got plenty of time to do whatever we want. All the time in the world."

"Sure we have."

In the quiet blackness of night, with the adults asleep and the desert only answering with a light whisper of wind, there was nothing or no one to contradict the boys' hopes. Overhead, cold distant stars filled the sky from horizon to horizon. The night was mute.

12

SHREVE WEST'S BETTER JOB FOR the summer meant loading watermelons onto flatbed trucks in the 115-degree heat instead of weeding cotton with a short-handled hoe in the 115-degree heat. It was a distinction that might have escaped most people, but for him the difference between the two jobs was clear.

Flinging or catching watermelons all day was preferable to the back spasms you got weeding cotton. Pitching watermelons felt like a sport same as lifting weights. Being big and strong, he took pride in being just as good with the watermelons as he was at the real sports he'd starred in for Cotton High. He could work all day, ten to twelve hours, sweating like a pig and enjoy himself the whole time.

He teased and goaded the other workers, a mixture of *braceros* and burly, local boys like himself, into frenzies of watermelon loading and stacking. Even his boss, fault-finding Jeff Clayborn, had trouble finding fault with him. But Jeff worked at it and somehow managed. That was the only part of the job Shreve didn't like—being bugged by his so-called boss.

"Them melons ain't gonna make it to the highway stacked like that, let alone to Indio. Shit, boy, look at 'em."

Shreve didn't go for much of that bull. He ignored Jeff as long as he could and when he couldn't, he talked back. Asked him to come up and stack the damn things himself. Asked him who the hell he thought did the work anyway. Usually Jeff stalked off and then grumbled about bad help. Other times it came close to a fight, but never the real thing.

It all started on Shreve's first day, and continued, usually once or twice a day. Shreve figured Jeff was stupid to spend all his time watching him when he had a wife like Marcie at home and no real reason to stay out in the fields ignoring her. Regardless, it seemed like Jeff had it in for Shreve and spent all his time watching to see if he screwed up.

During these days, somebody else was also keeping tabs on Shreve. Old King Cotton had heard rumors about his son-in-law's new hired hand and the old man began watching the watermelon crew from a distance—just to see for himself.

One typically baking hot day with triple digit heat and single digit humidity, and after one of the boss-worker run-ins, Shreve was getting a drink from a big aluminum water cooler when old man Cotton walked up. Jeff was a couple of rows away, sulking and kicking dirt clods with his cowboy boots.

"How you doing, boy?"

"Afternoon, Mr. Cotton." Shreve noticed the other loaders slow down to watch. Jeff turned his back as if pretending he wasn't trying to hear what they were saying.

"Hot enough out here for you fellows?" It was the standard question for this or virtually any other time of the year in the valley.

"Just right, sir, for jack rabbits and rattlesnakes."

King laughed. Jeff turned toward the distant mountains. The crew resumed working, but at a slower pace, still hoping to hear.

"Well, son, you planning to go to school this fall?"

"I been thinking some about Valley, sir, but I ain't made my mind up yet."

"Valley's loss and our gain if you don't. Can you drive a tractor?"

"If it's got wheels and a motor, I can drive it."

"How would you like to drive for me? Pays a damn sight more than chunking watermelons."

"Well." Shreve drawled. It might not be good form to accept too quickly a job he immediately knew he was going to.

"Well?" King bit off a small chew from a plug of Day's Work.

"Yes, sir, I'm your man."

"Good, you start tomorrow. Jeff will tell you where."

Shreve and the loaders looked over at Jeff. He had a grimace on his face like he'd eaten a *jalapeño* sandwich and downed it with a glass of Tabasco sauce. Shreve repressed a desire to howl with laughter. Some of his fellow workers didn't show the same restraint.

"Thank you, Mr. Cotton."

King Cotton didn't say anything else. He just wheeled and strode away, Jeff in his wake. There was a general celebration among the workers.

"I don't see why you went and promoted that West boy like that." Jeff complained to his father-in-law as they walked out of the field toward King's pickup.

"Why shouldn't I have?" King spit tobacco juice into the dusty road beside the field.

"He ain't worked here long enough."

"Hell, if you go by that, ain't nobody ever worked here long enough. That's the way farm work is. Nobody stays with it but idiots and bullheaded old men."

"I still don't like it." Jeff cocked his head to one side as if he weren't sure he belonged to the latter group and wondering if King had just put him into the former.

"Tell me why."

"He's got an attitude problem."

"An attitude problem? He's the hardest worker out here. You got something personal against him?"

"Naw, I just don't think he's the right man, that's all."

"Well, I do." King gave Jeff the straight in the eye look that had gained King the advantage in so many a farming deal over the years. "I do, and that's that. Hire him, pay him a fair tractor driver rate, and put him to work. If he don't work out—fair and square, none of your farting around—then you'll get to fire him. Any more objections?"

"No, sir."

That was as good a compromise as you were going to get out of King Cotton. Jeff knew the old man tolerated him and gave him more breaks than he did other people because of Marcie. He had accepted that a long time ago, but his ambitious nature tended to rear up when he least wanted it to and left him feeling used and second rate around the powerful Cotton patriarch. More like a Mexican irrigator than a son-in-law.

"Then do it."

King climbed into his pickup and drove off without looking back. Jeff swung his arm around in the dust cloud the pickup left behind.

"Damn it," he cursed. "Son of a bitch."

13

DARN, CATES." FRANK GRIPED TO Richard as they walked back in the dark from Cotton's migrant worker section northeast of the tracks. "We come all the way over here and the jerk ain't even home."

"Maybe we should have called first."

"He ain't got a phone."

"Oh, yeah, I forgot."

They neared the highway dividing the poor migrant area from the poor black area. "Well, what do you want to do? I hate not to do nothing on a Friday night."

"Listen." In the weak light of a rare street lamp, Richard put an index finger to his lips.

"What? What is it?"

"Can't you hear it?"

"That music?"

"Yeah."

"It's coming from the colored church." Frank pointed down the road to the left. The little church was all lit up inside and was expelling its excess of spirited singing and praising the Lord into the calm evening air.

"The negro church. Let's go look in."

"What for? I don't want to go peeping on 'em."

"Come on, it'll be neat."

"I don't like church. I ain't interested in it."

"This is different. Their church is different. They sing and dance. It's like a. . . a celebration."

"I don't know."

"Hey, we'll be able to see Reverend Wilcox in action."

"I see him every day just about. His apartment's right down the hall."

"I know but you've never see him preaching. We'll just look in for a little bit and then take off, okay? Then look for Cates or Shreve up town."

"Okay."

The music and praying and singing grew louder and louder as they approached the little white church. Up by a side window where they peered in, the boys could see Reverend Wilcox behind the pulpit.

"Look." Richard whispered as a particularly raucous, lively hymn came to an end. "Reverend Wilcox is starting to preach. He really puts himself into it."

Frank peeked in, hoping they wouldn't get caught out there where they didn't belong. He could pick up snatches of the reverend's sermon, which was punctuated by frequent cries of "amen" and "hallelujah."

"Our people have suffered long and. . . our brother Reverend King says. . . Birmingham and Oxford."

"He sure is a lot more fiery than when you see him uptown, isn't he?"

"He's always real polite to me and my mom."

"Look up front, there's Sandra. Man, is she pretty. And smart, too."

"You think so?"

"What?"

"Pretty."

"God, yes, don't you?"

"I never thought of her that way."

"Oh, yeah." Richard sniffed. "I forgot, you Southerners can't see anything but the color."

"That ain't true. I don't think that. I. . . ."

Suddenly two bright beams of light shone on the boys. They spun around, facing the blinding headlights of a car. They squinted to see who it was. A familiar voice called out from the dark.

"Hey, what the hell are you boys doing over there?"

"Shreve!" Richard exclaimed.

"Don't yell." Frank hissed through closed teeth. "Jeez, they're gonna hear us."

He looked back at the church and could see some of the parishioners turning to look toward the commotion.

"What you looking for in there," another familiar voice questioned loudly from the blackness behind the headlights, "some coon poon?"

"Oh, no." Frank groaned.

"For crying out loud, Cates. You got the attitudes of a spastic."

"Let's get out of here."

Frank rushed past Richard toward the car. Richard was right behind him. They piled into the back seat of Cates' Mercury, knocking their knees together.

"Ow." Richard yelped.

"Dang." Frank looked up to see Cates and Shreve looking at him. "What are you guys doing here? Those people are gonna be really pissed at us. Come on, let's get out of here."

"Well, what were you doing over there anyway? You don't belong here. What the hell were you up to?"

"I don't know what we were doing."

"We were watching the negro church service." Richard explained. "And for your information, it was interesting and fun."

"Martin, you talk like a damn book. Like you were doing an experiment for Mr. Davis. Those are real people."

"We didn't mean nothing, Shreve. We just wanted to watch."

"Big deal, Mason. You two ain't nothing but a couple of peeping Toms. You boys are weird."

"Okay, let's go. I feel plenty stupid."

"If I was driving, I'd dump the whole lot of you on the church steps and leave you to the mercy of the reverend."

"Sometimes you're a real jerk, Shreve." Cates was a little miffed. "It's my car. You ain't always in charge of everything."

"I'll feel like a jerk if the reverend sees me. I live right next to him. He's always been nice to me."

"We're all jerks, Frank." Richard commented. "That's what Cotton produces."

"Hit it, Cates." Shreve ordered. "Here comes somebody."

Cates slammed the Mercury into gear and hammered the gas. They spun around, rocks and dust flying, and shot out onto the highway just as the front door of the church opened and a couple of men poked their heads out. Frank ducked down in the seat and closed his eyes.

14

IT TOOK A GLORIOUS, BRIGHT blue summer Saturday, three hours on a gently rocking Salton Sea, and the landing of a ten-pound corvina for Frank to lose the sheepishness he still felt about spying on Reverend Wilcox's church service. The fish, easily many times bigger than any Frank ever caught before, finally wiped out the rest of the bad feelings. Now he felt good, and proud, his bleeding knuckles and cramped fingers bearing witness to the fish's fight for freedom and Frank's lack of skill as a fisherman. Uncle Carl Waters had talked him through the catch and had gotten a big charge out of his scrawny nephew's success.

"That's a good 'un," he must have repeated five times, even though he had caught three corvina nearly twice as big as Frank's, "a real big one. Boy, that'll taste good when the old woman cooks that tonight, won't it? Boy, that's a good 'un."

Frank gouged another mudsucker onto his hook and got off a good cast, sending the line far from the boat. The bait landed intact and where he wanted it to, just to the right of some above-water limbs of a submerged tree.

"How about another drink?" Uncle Carl sat in the front seat of the boat. "We got any cold ones left?"

"Sure, that'd go good right now, wouldn't it?"

Frank reached into a big cooler and got an ice cold Coors for Uncle Carl, a nearly frozen Coke for himself. Carl took a big swig of the beer and Frank imagined eating the corvina that night, cooked to a T by his Aunt Jean and, with a little catsup on it, melting in his mouth. He took a long drink of Coke and leaned back in the thick-cushioned portable chair Uncle Carl provided for fishing guests. Feeling content and comfortable, he sipped on his Coke and daydreamed.

The Coke reminded him of his last semester at Cotton High, when he and Cates and a couple of buddies started spiking their lunch time Cokes with gin and vodka they smuggled back from Mexicali in the trunk of Cates' car. They would get a small buzz from the alcohol but act more affected than they really were. The booze did improve his accent in the afternoon Spanish class though.

While the boat rocked and his line bobbed, he became aware of a humming sound somewhere to his left. It took a minute to extricate himself from a pleasant memory of his former girlfriend, Annie Bishop, before he realized the humming noise was another boat passing relatively nearby on the spacious inland saltwater sea.

"There goes old King Cotton, himself." Carl pointed at the other boat. "With his daughter and that son-in-law of his."

The woman waved and Frank waved to her. The old man gave them a wave of his straw hat. The other man didn't look over as the large powerboat zipped by. The big boat's wake sent several waves at Carl and Frank's boat, the water slapping against the side and causing it to rock back and forth for several moments. Frank watched the passing boat until it was a light spot against the bright horizon.

"Uncle Carl," he kept an eye out at his slack line and reeled it in some, "did you ever work for King Cotton?"

"Sure did. Shoot, I reckon everybody around here worked for old King one time or another. All the older men anyway. Can't say about you younger fellas. But I suspect a good amount of them, too."

"My friend Shreve's working for him now."

"He's a good enough boss, kinda rough around the edges, but pays a fair wage for a fair day's work."

"Was Cotton named after him?"

Carl tossed his empty beer can back to Frank, who dropped it in the cooler and took out another. Carl popped a hole in the top with a church key, making a small air hole opposite the large drinking one. He took a swallow and sighed.

"Boy, that's good." He set the beer down and fussed with his line a moment. "What was that again?"

"Was Cotton named after Mr. Cotton there?"

"No, it was his grandpa. Come in here before there even was a Salton Sea."

"Wow, way back, huh?"

"Yep, back a good spell all right."

"Was he a farmer, too?"

"Yeah, and a big farmer, too. Come out from Texas with a lot of money and a lot of spunk. Built up a hell of a spread here in the north end."

"Like it is now?"

"Probably bigger, but his son, King's daddy, lost a lot of it. You might have heard about him."

"No, not really."

Frank reeled in his bait-less line. He hadn't even felt the nibbles that had cleaned the little fish off his hook. He got out another mudsucker and baited the hook again.

"It's funny, I've been here for a couple of years but I don't know much about the Cottons. They're too rich I reckon. And the kids are older'n me. Like Mrs. Clayborn and Billy."

"Well, King's daddy liked his whiskey and he liked his women." Carl continued as Frank cast his line out by the sunken tree again. "After the old grandfather died, the son let everything go to hell. Wasn't till King got grown and the war started that they really built back up. He had a big old chunk of land up by Northland and he sold it to the Army to build a training base."

"During World War II?"

"Yep. World War II. Old King took that money and bought up all the land he could and farmed it. He took over everything his father left behind and built up the family's land to nearly what it was to start with."

"Man, oh, man, they're really rich, aren't they?"

"You bet."

"Wow."

"The only screw-up was King's daughter marrying that Jeff Clayborn. He's just low-down mean. Treats his help bad. Don't see what that girl sees in him anyway. You work for his brother Buck, don't you?"

"Yeah. Not much improvement there either, I tell you. But, boy, that Mrs. Clayborn is really pretty, isn't she?"

"You ain't just a whistling Dixie, she's—whoa, watch it there, man. You got something."

"Huh?" Frank looked up to see his line dip well under the surface. He jerked hard and started reeling in the line.

"Slow up, easy, easy, you got him."

"It's a big one. Really big. Bigger'n the other one."

"Bring him in easy. Slow and easy."

Frank kept pulling and reeling in the line. Carl tried to slow him down. Frank fought and fought, dragging the fish, a huge corvina he guessed from the weight and the fight, toward the boat. It was the biggest fish he'd ever hooked.

"Not so rough. Gentle, smooth, strong."

Frank pulled with all his might and the line went slack. He pitched backward, almost falling overboard, causing the boat to rock wildly.

"Shit."

He quickly looked over at his uncle, who showed neither shock nor surprise. Instead he got so tickled he dropped his beer.

"Shit."

"Heck. I guess I really blew that one."

With considerable effort, Carl finally managed to stop laughing.

"I reckon so." His face wrinkled up in a broad smile. "I reckon so."

15

CAROL SCOTT DIDN'T KNOW WHY she'd agreed to go for a drive with Lar Turner but here they were parked on a dirt hill overlooking the Salton Sea. They were well off the road and the fading light of day ensured that no one out on the road could easily identify who was in the car, but she feared someone would see them, anyway.

Between that worry and her physical proximity to Lar, she felt jumpy. She figured he didn't care much for nervousness in a woman, but also figured his hopes for a big night might help him make the effort to be tolerant.

"Stop fidgeting, nobody can see us up here. Look how the sea looks in this light—like the end of a Gene Autry movie, ain't it?"

Actually, it didn't remind her of a Gene Autry movie at all. She didn't go to the movies that often anymore, much less to see Gene Autry. Besides, he was a cowboy and she doubted his movies ever ended with him staring off at the Salton Sea.

Before Billy Cotton left she used to go to the movies with him over in Brawley and El Centro, but even those bored her and she usually fell asleep halfway through. She would like to enjoy movies like everybody else but she just couldn't. They were too boring.

"Gene Autry was a cowboy." She smoothed out a fold in her skirt. "I don't see what it's got to do with the Salton Sea." Lar scratched his head and gave her an annoyed look.

"Damn."

"Don't curse."

"Shit, I ain't cussing."

"There, you did it again."

"Just come here." He reached his arm around Carol's shoulders and pulled her, resisting, to him. "C'mon, be nice. You know I like you."

He held her close and kissed her on the cheek, then struggled to kiss her mouth. Carol pulled back, freed herself.

"What's wrong?"

"Nothing."

"Then, why'd you pull away?"

"I don't know."

"Is it me? What'd I do? What?"

"No, it's not you."

"Who then? Not him again? If you want to be with him, why are you with me? He's not coming back."

Carol lowered her head. She still thought of herself as Billy Cotton's girl. He had been gone a long time. Maybe Lar was right. Maybe Billy wasn't coming back. A girl couldn't wait forever. Marcie sure wouldn't. And Lar was there beside her. Strong and not bad looking, he wanted her and he was a grown man. Billy was strong and handsome, but he was a boy—and he wasn't there beside her. No, Billy Cotton wasn't the only reason she was slow warming up.

"It isn't Billy, either." She looked shyly at Lar. "It's me. I don't know what's wrong with me."

Lar pulled her to him. This time she didn't resist.

"Naw, baby." He soothed. "You ain't done nothing wrong. You're a good girl."

"Am I?"

"Yes, sure you are."

She felt his right arm close around her shoulder, nearly touching her breast. Her heart raced and her breath came short and shallow. He played with her hair and kissed her lightly on the temple. She tried to think of Billy Cotton but she could only imagine the outline of his face.

Lar's kisses became more frequent, urgent. His hands touched her where Billy's hadn't. She didn't want to give in, but she grew tired of the tussle. Tired of waiting for a boy who might never come back, tired of always being in control, especially tired of being a good girl. It was all too hard. Too tiring. She leaned back in the seat and let Lar do what he wanted.

"Please, baby." He groaned, clumsily unbuttoning her blouse.

Carol felt the air on her bare skin and leaned back. His weight pushed her down awkwardly in the seat. His breath was hot, his kisses rough against her breasts. She looked up at the roof of the car and closed her eyes while he did his business with her body. She felt as if she were far away, oddly uninvolved. Even the pain seemed to belong to someone else. She turned her head away. In a few minutes he was done.

On the drive back into Cotton they didn't speak. He dropped her off at home and drove away without a word. She soaked in the tub for an hour, then went to bed and cried herself to sleep.

Damn Billy Cotton for leaving her.

16

NORTHLAND WAS SMALLER THAN COTTON, not half as big. With the exception of Red Becker's bar three blocks into town on the northeast side, every business in town lay on a two hundred yard strip down both sides of the highway. Rumbling semis and speeding travelers raced past the dusty settlement of three or four streets without a second glance.

Out on the highway, the west strip of businesses included a busy bait shop, a small market, a smaller five and dime, and a tiny dry cleaner. The east side had a larger market, a cafe, a small hardware store, a dinky little bar, and the post office. Across the corner from the post office sat Northland's most successful concern—Galvan's Restaurant and Filling Station.

Galvan's was the town's gathering place for a mixture of locals, a few regular truck drivers, and folks up from Cotton. Wanda Pate, forty-five, heavy, amiable, gum-smacking waitress, was ringing up Shreve and Frank's bill when Cates pulled up outside.

"That's a dollar seventy-five, boys." She chomped her gum. They counted out the money and handed it to her. Outside, Cates honked his horn. "Your friend acts like he's in a hurry, boys."

"You know Cates. He's always on his own planet."

"He is a character. Well, thank you, boys, come again."

"Okay, Wanda."

Shreve walked ahead and left a quarter tip on their table. Frank pitched in a dime.

"Tell your mama hi for me." Wanda called as the boys headed out the door.

In the parking lot, Cates motioned for them to join him in his Mercury.

"Just leave your pickup here, Shreve." Cates leaned over the rider's seat to be heard. "Come on with me."

"Sounds like a deal."

They piled into the Merc, Shreve riding shotgun, Frank in back. They barely sat down before Cates started delivering the latest news.

"Did you hear about Lonnie Bass?" He pulled the gearshift toward him and up into reverse.

"What about him?"

"He got killed this afternoon." Cates backed the Mercury onto Palm Street and headed east toward Red Becker's.

"That's awful."

"This better not be one of your dumb rumors."

"No way, Shreve, my dad heard it in Cotton from Manny Ruiz. Lonnie was flagging for a crop duster and it hit and killed him."

"Oh, jeez." Frank shook his head. "That's terrible."

"A wheel knocked his head off."

"Darn, he was in Billy Cotton's class at school wasn't he?"

"Yeah." Cates confirmed. "They were older'n us."

"I didn't know him well."

"I swear those damn things get somebody—a pilot or flagman—killed about ever' six months."

"That's right."

"Doesn't anybody ever try to do something about it?" Frank wondered.

"Naw not really. Sometimes somebody'll make a fuss for a while but nothing ever changes. Nobody gives a damn about duster pilots out here, and sure as hell not about flaggers."

"What a lousy way to go." Frank shuddered, picturing the biplane's wheel smacking into Lonnie Bass' head.

"You can say that again." Cates turned south on California Street and headed toward the Northland Community Church. "Real bad. Don't you think so, Shreve?"

"Ain't no good way. But whatever gets you, gets you. That's the name of that story."

"Ain't you scared of dying, Shreve? Don't you think about it?"

"Not much. Heck, Frankie, we just graduated from high school. What do I want to think about dying for? There's too much living to do yet to worry about that BS."

"It can happen any time to anybody, my old man always says." Cates looked over at Shreve. "He says it's in God's hands."

"When your number's up, it's up. That's all."

"Maybe so." Frank was pensive. He looked out the window just as they were passing the Community Church. The building where he had attended Sunday school and church services during his first year in the valley. It was unlit and empty, fragile, with the paint peeling off the old, warping wood. It didn't look at all like the house of an omniscient, omnipotent, and omnipresent God—the Temple of the Lord. He looked away.

"Come on, you guys, let's go get a Coke and drive around the other part of town some more. Okay?"

"Sounds good." Cates revved up the Merc.

"Let's do it." Shreve pointed at the road ahead.

17

THE BOYS MADE SEVERAL PASSES through town without running into anybody they knew. They turned down a side street a block or two from a handful of empty buildings that constituted the original, "old" Northland. Out on the front porch of a little cracker box white wood house they saw a tall, well-built blonde girl watering pots of flowers.

"Look, Mason." Cates acted excited. "There she is."

"Who? Who?"

"On the left, up there. It's Karen Edwards."

"Oh, my."

Karen was a sophomore, to be a junior in the fall, and Frank had had an unrequited crush on her since his first summer in the valley when he and his mother had lived for a short time in Northland. Karen had been a gangly fourteen-going-on-fifteen then, now she was sixteen going on full-grown. He liked her well enough, but he could never muster the courage to approach her. She was too much for him. He could only admire her from a distance.

"She might be the best looking girl in CHS." Shreve judged as they slowly passed by.

"She's really stacked." Cates leered.

Karen looked up and gave them a wave and a broad, white smile. Frank felt light-headed looking at that smile. He figured if it was ever directed exclusively at him, he'd just flop right down and die.

"Sweet Jesus."

"Don't go getting religious on me now, boy." Shreve joked.

"Lord, she's pretty." Frank looked out the back window as they drove on.

Karen had turned away and now watered plants on the other side of the porch. Frank said a little secular prayer that she might be at Cotton's Fourth of July celebration coming up in a couple of days.

"Want me to go back and you can talk to her?"

"No, no, don't you dare, Cates. I'll kill you."

"Ooh, I'm scared."

"You're a puss, Mason." Shreve slapped back at Frank from the front seat. "A pussy-whipped punk." Frank punched him on the arm.

"What a tough guy." Shreve feigned a punch which Frank pretended to block.

"We're getting hot now." Cates announced as they pulled up to the stop sign where Karen's street intersected with Palm—Red Becker's bar was on the opposite corner.

A dark-haired muscular man in western clothes and shiny-clean cowboy boots walked out of Red Becker's with a small-breasted, well-dressed, but overly made up woman. When they got close to a big white Oldsmobile, the man swatted the woman on the rear. She jumped and squealed.

"It's Jeff Clayborn." Frank couldn't hide his surprise. He knew Jeff Clayborn was a regular at Reverend Kincaid's Community Church less than three blocks away. He also knew Jeff was married to Marcie Cotton. "Can you believe that?"

"That boy's an absolute fool." Shreve was disgusted. "He's got Marcie Cotton at home and he's running around with some whore."

"You don't know she's a whore, Shreve."

"Maybe not, Jimbo, but she's made up like one and she's with Jeff Clayborn."

"Boy, what a phony." Frank used one of Richard Martin's favorite words. "Goes to church and then runs around on Marcie. I don't like that guy. I don't like that kind of crap."

The big Olds passed by the boys.

"I'll have to be on my toes now." Shreve whistled. "That bastard must've seen me and he'll try to get me in trouble with old King."

"The way you tell it." Cates turned the Merc west toward the highway. "Old King loves you."

Up ahead, Jeff Clayborn's Olds was already nearly to the highway.

"I intend to keep it that way. If I'm gonna get ahead in Cotton, I need the old man's backing. It's his crop, his name, his place."

"Buck Clayborn asked me if I would be a caretaker and work out at one of Jeff's orchard farms in the desert out here," Frank revealed to his buddies. "I start a couple of weeks after the Fourth. What do you guys think of that?"

"By yourself?" Cates turned south back toward the Community Church.

"In the daytime I'll work with a couple of other guys, at night I'm by myself."

"Shit, Mason, you'll be so scared out there you'll pee your pants."

"I will not, Shreve. I can do it."

"Sure you can, as long as there ain't any ghosts or vampires roaming the desert out there."

"Shoot."

"It could be cool." Cates made the first right past the church. "Nobody around to bug you all the time."

"Yeah."

"Damn straight." Cates slipped into a terrible Bela Lugosi imitation. "Real quiet and peaceful. Nothing but howling coyotes and the moans of the un-dead—bluh, bluh." Shreve and Frank laughed.

Cates stopped at the highway, then made a right toward Galvan's. Shreve leaned his head out the window and let the wind blow in his face. In the back seat, Frank mentally pictured a vampire sucking blood from his throat.

"Listen, guys." Cates turned back east into town. "I got some other news besides poor old Lonnie."

"What news?" Shreve sounded suspicious.

"What about?" Frank wrenched himself free from the image of a beautiful vampire he'd conjured in his mind.

"About the valley."

"The valley?" Frank wondered. "The whole valley?"

"All of it."

"Oh, crap." Shreve frowned. "Here it comes. Get your hip boots on, Mason. It's about to get deep."

"They're gonna make this movie about the valley." Cates explained. "It's all about the people who came out here during the Depression."

"The Dust Bowl Okies."

Shreve turned around, aimed a finger at Frank and acted like he fired a pistol.

"You're always on it, Mason."

"They all came out here looking for work." Frank elaborated. "A lot of them stopped here in the valley."

"Your uncle for one."

"Uh-huh."

"Yeah, well, that's it. They're coming here to film."

"Cates." Shreve snorted. "You are so full of bull that there ain't a cow pie left in the entire valley."

"Hey, I swear it's true. Maybe they'll film here in Northland."

"Right."

"You know that's a funny name for this place, Northland. Northland. Why do you suppose they called it that? It's basically at the southeast end of the Salton Sea—at least sort of. Seems odd don't it?"

"Cates." Shreve made a clucking sound. "You kill me. Why is it Northland? Why is the damn sky blue? You know why? Because it's at the north end of the damned Imperial County. That's all. Ain't nothing else to it."

"I swear, Shreve, you ain't got no imagination at all."

"Go to hell."

Cates feigned hurt. "Well, since you all don't believe nothing I ever say. I guess it's time for me to drop you off at Galvan's."

"Yeah, we gotta get back to Cotton anyway. Right, Frankie?"

"Couldn't we make one more run by Red's?"

"Red's? What for? Oh, I get it."

"Pussy-whipped, pussy-whipped." Shreve taunted Frank.

"Frank and Karen sitting in a tree. . . ." Cates joined in.

"Ah, jeez." Frank blushed.

But Cates headed toward the street where Karen Edwards lived just down from Red Becker's bar. Frank rested his head on his left hand and looked out the window. The Mercury's oversized engine rumbled loudly as the boys cruised along Northland's quiet streets. It was another hot day in the valley.

18

WONDERFUL JOB, REVEREND WILCOX." NANCY Ruglia complimented her guest speaker. She held sway as the current president of the North Valley Women's Society, a philanthropic group made up of fifteen to twenty of the more liberal wives of well-to-do north end farmers and businessmen. "I'm sure all the girls were as moved as I was."

"I thank you, Mrs. Ruglia. It was most generous of you all to invite me."

Most of the ladies had gathered in the back of Cotton's American Legion Hall for punch and cookies, but several, including Marcie Clayborn and a tubby lady named Fanny, had joined Nancy in a circle around the reverend.

"We think it's wonderful you're doing such good work with the, with your people." Fanny flashed a fleshy smile. "It's important for God's love to be spread among those who haven't been as blessed as the rest of us."

Marcie cocked her head toward Fanny, but Fanny didn't let on that she saw.

"It does sound like a promising project, Mr. Wilcox." Marcie turned her attention to the reverend and bestowed on him one of her highest-powered smiles. "*Very* promising."

"Very kind of you, Mrs. Clayborn. We believe a new Sunday School building is just what our young folk need. Nowadays, the young people need more help from their elders than they did in less confusing times."

"You're so right, Reverend Wilcox." Fanny chimed in. "Children today grow up too fast, why in our day—"

"I think," Marcie interrupted, "the best part of all is putting in a kitchen to feed the families who are having a bad time of it. Don't you agree, Fanny?"

"Uh, why, yes, I do."

"And any needy family is welcome to the Sunday meal, is that right?" Nancy spoke up. "Even the seasonal workers?"

"Yes, ma'am, of course. The Lord's house is always open to the humble and the meek. Both the Sunday School and the kitchen would be for all to share who need it. That's the Christian way."

"Wonderful. It sounds like a real good thing."

"Quite American, too." Fanny interjected. "So appropriate with the Fourth coming up Thursday."

"It does sound good. So what are we going to do about it? Congratulate Reverend Wilcox and send him on his way?"

Marcie raised her voice so the ladies in back could hear over their munching and sipping.

"Girls, we've got an opportunity to do something useful for a change. Are we here to shovel the food in or help those in our own community who need it?"

The ladies by the punch bowl looked up, surprised.

Reverend Wilcox focused on the wall plaques honoring Cotton's war dead. His eyes strayed across one engraved with the name Johnny D. Waters.

"Well?" Marcie insisted. The ladies stared at her. "Okay, I'll start."

She reached in her purse and pulled out a checkbook. The reverend tactfully continued his study of the walls. Marcie wrote a check, ripped it out of the book and handed it to Reverend Wilcox.

"That'll get you started."

"Thank you, Mrs. Clayborn. You don't know how much this means."

"I'm sure you'll use it well, Mr. Wilcox."

The other ladies began digging for checkbooks. There were a few frowns aimed at Marcie. When all the donations were collected, Fanny timidly pulled Marcie out of earshot of the others.

"Marcie, don't take this wrong, but I don't think the other girls liked being forced to donate to the reverend's cause."

"Forced? Is that what happened? I put a gun to everyone's head and made them write a check? If they didn't want to give they didn't have to."

"But you're so, so—*dominate*."

"Dominant, you mean? You make me sound like a bully or something."

"Well. . . ."

"Fanny, darling, if I didn't push and bully you girls, you'd never get anything done. All you'd ever do is organize barbecues and luaus."

"You could try being nicer about it."

Marcie looked into Fanny's green eyes set deep behind her chubby cheeks and put a hand on her pudgy forearm.

"Sure, hon, I'll try to be nicer. I'll make it a Fourth of July resolution."

Fanny giggled nervously. Marcie patted her on the hand.

"Now, I've got to run. I'll see you Thursday night."

Fanny gave a little wave and watched Marcie walk over by the door where Reverend Wilcox stood talking to a couple of the ladies.

"Excuse me. I'm sorry, but I've got to run over to El Centro for some things for the Fourth of July show up at the school. Thanks again, Mr. Wilcox, and best of luck with your project."

"Thank you, Mrs. Clayborn." The reverend bowed. "You're most generous."

"Think nothing of it. Glad to be of some help."

Those remaining watched until the classic contours of Marcie Cotton Clayborn's form disappeared into the hot afternoon beyond the air conditioned walls of the Legion hall.

"That's quite a lady."

"Indeed, Reverend." One of the ladies sniffed. "Quite a lady indeed."

19

I'VE GOT A SURPRISE FOR everyone in my speech tomorrow night up at school." Teddy Martinez informed Jean Waters while she sold him a dozen five-cent stamps.

"Is that right?" Jean tore the stamps from a shiny new sheet and handed them to Teddy.

"And what exactly is that surprise going to be?"

"Can't tell, of course, wouldn't be a surprise."

"Well, aren't you a stinker." Jean looked past Teddy to see her sister Kate Mason entering the post office.

It was near noon and Kate usually dropped by to see Jean on her way back to York's Electric after lunch. These days Kate anticipated the mail more than usual—she and Jean had begun submitting poetry to small magazines and Kate waited to hear back on several submissions.

"Hello, Mr. Theodore." Kate adopted a playful formality she and Teddy used whenever they ran into one another. "Hi, Jean."

"Hi, sis."

"Good day to you, Mrs. Mason. A fine day, is it not?"

"Why, yes, it is. You're certainly chipper today. Something special happen?"

"He's got a surprise for us at the Fourth show tomorrow."

"Oh, now what could that be, *Señor* Martinez?"

"Can't tell." Teddy dropped sixty cents on the counter and took his stamps. "You'll have to wait till tomorrow night." He headed for the door.

"In that case, I'll have to wait even later. I'm working at Galvan's tomorrow night. I won't be making it to the fireworks show."

"Too bad, I guess Jean'll have to, oops. . . ."

He trailed off midsentence when a tall, thick, older man stomped through the half open door. From the man's purposeful stride and air of detachment, it was clear he was a man accustomed to being in charge.

"Uh, good day, Mr. Cotton." Teddy spoke to the man's back.

Jean and Kate watched the big man walk toward the locked mailboxes down the small side corridor beside the mail window.

"Good day," he grunted.

From the door, Teddy winked at the women and went out shaking his head.

"How are you today, Mr. Cotton?" King didn't respond, he was already in the back banging around on his mailbox. "Still nothing today." Jean then turned to Kate, anticipating her sister's query.

"This waiting is the worst part. Do they always take so long to write back?"

"Often, but when they do take one of your poems, it makes all the waiting worthwhile."

"I can only hope for that day."

"It'll come."

King Cotton came back up front and stood across from the stamp window appearing to scan through his mail. The women watched him for a moment.

"Can I help you, Mr. Cotton?"

"Uh, no." King appeared to be his usual grumpy self.

The sisters found his attitude amusing. To them, he was just an old Okie farm boy who'd almost gotten too big for his breeches. He looked from his mail to Kate.

"York gonna be back at the store today?"

"He'll be back late this afternoon. He's out at the Navy air base on a big job."

"What time he be back?"

"After four, I suspect."

"You open till then?"

"No, sir, I'm working up at Galvan's tonight and Matthew told me to close early. We'll be open until about three-thirty."

"You work two jobs, Mrs. Mason, to take care of yourself and that boy of yours? Don't he do nothing?"

"He's working for Buck Clayborn now, Mr. Cotton." She didn't know he knew anything about her or Frank.

"Well, he oughta be. Hard working woman like yourself needs some help ever now an' agin. I wonder you don't have a man to look out for you. Young woman like yourself."

"Why, Mr. Cotton." Kate blushed. Jean busied herself behind the counter.

"It ain't good for a woman to be left alone without a man."

Kate was speechless. Old Cotton looked out the front window. He coughed and with a mumbled "goodbye ladies" headed for the door. No one had ever accused him of cultivating the social graces. His brief forays into civilization were like the dust devils that sprung up on the alkaline soil of his thousands of acres of desert land—unexpected, swirling, and over as fast as they started. Leaving everything in their wake feeling a little overwhelmed. The women watched him go.

"My word, was that a tornado come through here or what? Why, I swear Katherine, I do believe that man flirted with you."

"Lord, I hope not. No, of course he wasn't."

"Can you imagine that, the biggest man in the valley interested in my little sister?"

"Hush now. Don't you dare say anything like that. My goodness, if that was to get around, I could never live it down."

"If it was true, you wouldn't have to live it down. You could live it up from now on."

Kate giggled and put her hand over her mouth. Jean started laughing, too.

"You are so bad." Kate joked with her big sister. "Just awful. I'm going back to work."

"Better keep your eye peeled for celebrity customers this afternoon."

"You keep yours peeled looking for my good luck letter now."

"Okay, kid. See you later."

"Bye-bye."

Kate opened the door into the seemingly perpetual blast of Imperial Valley heat and stepped out onto the scorched sidewalk. She looked both ways for any sign of King, but he was already gone. With a light step she turned left and hurried on to York's.

20

FRANK STOOD IN THE CHECKOUT line at Manny Ruiz's with a warm six-pack of Pepsi to put in the refrigerator for later and a frosty-cold cream soda for drinking as soon as he paid for it. He was tired and sweaty from another full day of fixing cotton picker spindles and was thinking the job in the desert Buck set him up with had to be better than repairing those idiotic spindles. The word cotton picker itself, once connoting fields of waving white bolls and the wonder of modern technology to Frank, now made him grimace. He was sure if he never saw another cotton picker it would be too damned soon.

"How's it going, Frank?" Manny rang up the sodas. "You want this one opened, or what?"

Frank handed over the cream soda and Manny popped the lid off on an opener mounted on the side of the checkout counter. He liked the affable store-owner, an old Cotton High athlete himself, because he had taken a liking to Frank's brand of relatively adroit—if undersized—football and baseball play, and had publicly complimented him on it.

"Thanks, Manny." He took a swig of the cream soda and retrieved the Pepsis from the counter.

"Big doings tomorrow night."

"You bet." Frank headed out of the store. "See you later."

"Okay."

Frank felt tired but good. It was a little lonely with his mother at work and his buddies off at their own jobs, but he didn't mind it so much some times. Out in front of the post office by the adjacent steps that led up to his apartment, he saw old Homer Cole, the town bum, digging in a filthy trashcan. Homer lived in a little ramshackle house off the alley in back of Ruiz's market, but he was most often seen, as now, raiding garbage cans in front of the businesses on Main Street. At times, he panhandled for enough change to buy food or a bottle, but those times were rare. He was a hermit living in a small town instead of a cave.

Frank ducked into the stairwell behind Homer and jogged up the steps to the landing at the beginning of the long, backwards L-shaped hallway leading to his and his mother's apartment. With the unexpected image of Karen Edwards playing in his mind's eye, he walked past the hot water heater closet where he ordinarily hid bottles of booze he and his pals occasionally brought back from Mexicali. A few feet down the hall on the left was Reverend Wilcox's apartment with, as usual, no light shining under the door. The reverend spent little time there, apparently filling the majority of his days in work for his church.

He was almost to the right turn in the hall, directly across from the door of the third apartment on the floor—the one where old man Pritchard died the night he and his semi-invalid wife had moved in, when suddenly, a large man with a severely cropped crew cut emerged from the shadows in front of the apartment. The man wore dark slacks, a stained white shirt, and a skinny black tie—the picture of rumpled officialdom and authority. Surprised, Frank almost dropped his cream soda.

"You live around here, fella?" The man grinned a toothy smile.

He seemed to be trying not to be too threatening. Frank wasn't keen on the situation. He felt like turning tail and running. The man seemed to sense this.

"It's okay, son, I just want to ask some questions. You live here?"

"Y—yes, sir."

"Colored preacher live back down the hallway there, does he?" The man pointed past Frank.

Frank resisted an urge to look around. He wished like anything that his mom wasn't doing another half-night shift for Galvan.

"Reverend Wilcox?"

"That's right."

"Did he do something?"

"You see him around much?"

"Ever' now and then."

"He ever with anybody else? Other colored men?"

"I never seen any. Why?"

"Official business, son. That's all you need to know."

"Did he commit some crime?"

"Leave the questions to me. How about women? Has he ever brought women up here?"

"No way. Never."

"Never held meetings or anything like that? No unusual number of visitors?"

"No, sir."

"Did he ever hand out pamphlets or literature about negro causes?"

"Not to me."

"You ever see him carrying pictures of Negro agitators or hear him talk about such things?"

"No." Frank lied.

He recalled the snatches of Reverend Wilcox's sermon he and Richard had heard just a few days before and was sure some of it might have to do with the "agitators" the big man referred to. But something made him say no. The big man was too narrow-eyed, or too nosy, or something. His questions made Frank feel like a snitch if he answered them. If there was one thing he didn't want to be, it was a snitch.

"No, I never heard or seen anything like that."

The burly man looked steadily at Frank's face. Frank tried to avoid meeting eyes without looking fidgety. After a moment the man seemed satisfied. He dropped his gaze and stepped by Frank into the main hallway.

"Okay, son, that's good. Your information has helped."

Frank wondered what information that was and what it helped. He just wished the guy would go away.

"I'm going to go now, but you have to promise me one thing." The man jabbed a finger at Frank, who rapidly nodded his assent. "Nobody knows we had this little talk."

"No, sir. Huh-uh."

"Atta boy. Official business."

"Official business."

The big man clapped him on the shoulder with a meaty hand and walked away. At the landing, he turned and looked back. Frank ducked out of sight by his door. He listened till he heard the man start down the stairs. When the door opened to the street below, he rushed into his apartment and locked the door. He set the sodas on the coffee table in front of the couch, which also served as his bed, and crept over to the window. Carefully pulling the curtain back, he looked for the man but didn't see anyone on the sidewalk except old man Cole who was going through garbage cans on the other side of the street.

After about five minutes, he did see a black, nondescript Ford coupe head out of town going south, but couldn't see who was driving. He kept up the vigil for about another half hour, until his fear that the burly man might return dissipated. With a sigh, he turned away from the window. His eyes immediately went to the sodas still on the coffee table

"Crap." He grabbed the Pepsis and hustled them to the refrigerator. "They'll never get cold now."

He went back to the living room and picked up the cream soda. It had been sitting there all that time without a cap. He took a tentative swig. It was warm already.

"Damn it. Big jerk nearly ruined my soda."

21

FRANK SPENT ALL DAY OF the Fourth in a state of paranoia over the "visit" of the burly man with the cheap clothes and the stubble-high crew cut. He hardly thought about the fireworks show—usually one of his favorite things in Cotton—at all.

After work he went back to the empty apartment, half expecting to see the man waiting in the hallway again, and listlessly forced down a plain bologna sandwich and half a glass of milk. Then he sat around on the couch staring at nothing until it was time to go to the show. He'd hardly seen anyone, neither his mother nor his friends, over the last couple of days, and he felt distant from others, out of kilter in general.

By the time he headed up to the CHS football field it was getting late. When he got there, it was dusk. Feeling alone and isolated, he came in from the back of the field by way of the baseball diamond, both fields still resonant of the games he'd played during his two years at Cotton High.

He went over to a concession stand, bought a Coke, and then hung to one side in back of the happy throng celebrating Independence Day. From the back he had a good view of the crowd, and he stood watching them as if they were in one world and he in another.

In the east end zone, firemen were preparing the display, helped by Mayor Lowell and Dale Honeycutt. Out on the dirt track Lar sat in a patrol car. He didn't appear to be doing anything. Near the front left of the crowd, Sandra Glover talked to Teddy Martinez and even in the failing light, Frank could tell they were having an animated conversation. For a split second he wondered what the two might be talking about so heatedly, and for a brief moment, the visages of Reverend Wilcox and the burly man who interrogated Frank flashed through his consciousness unbidden. To his relief, those images were quickly replaced by the actual sight of another familiar figure who now caught his attention.

It was Shreve, and he stood near to and was talking with Marcie Clayborn. What would they have to say to one another? Frank watched with interest as Jeff Clayborn popped up beside Marcie, and Shreve almost simultaneously drifted away into the shadows. Marcie always looked so cool and pretty and seeing her made Frank think of Karen Edwards. He had hoped to see Karen here but with it getting too dark and so hard to see, he gave up on the idea and let himself be swept away by the fireworks display.

For a little town, Cotton put on a good Fourth of July show. This year they even had some of the new sky rockets that fired twice, delivering a second explosion of color just before the first went out. The crowd "oohed and aahed" over those. Another new kind were the balls of flame that burst with the concussive power of a cannon blast. These came every fifth or sixth shot and they resounded with a powerful echo that could be heard over much of the north end of the valley.

During one of the loud boomers, while the field was still visible from the light, Frank looked down at the crowd and saw Annie Bishop not far in front of him. She happened to turn around just at that moment and as the night enveloped the field again they looked directly at each other. It had gotten too dark again too quickly for Frank to read her expression, but in his mood he imagined she had the same expression he'd seen on her face the last time they'd run into each other a few weeks before—a hurt, confused look.

Back in his senior year, for some reason he didn't understand himself, he had decided he no longer wanted to go with Annie. He wanted to be free— footloose and fancy-free was the old expression he remembered. So, without real cause he broke up with her and now he couldn't go back. The memory left him feeling melancholy and a little ashamed of himself. He just stared up into the night, watching the fireworks explode loudly and colorfully.

But unlike years past, the show brought him no great pleasure. He was just glad no one saw him there, saw him for who he really was. Some guy who hurt a nice girl for no reason whatsoever, except maybe for his own sense of being free—whatever that meant. He felt stupid, and glad for the dark, glad that, at least for the moment, his failings were hidden from the crowd, hidden from the light of day.

22

THE FIREWORKS SHOW WAS WELL along when Cates found Frank. Even in the poor light of the flaring skyrockets, he could see his friend looked a little forlorn. From two years of knowing him, Cates discovered that humor and enthusiasm could usually drag his buddy out of these occasional funks he drifted into.

"Hey," he called out with considerable gusto. "What's going on, pal? Great show, huh?"

"Yeah." Frank's voice sounded funny, weak. Cates recognized it as the one he'd heard before when Frank studied too long or had been by himself too much. "It's real good."

"Pretty cool about Teddy Martinez, huh?"

"What?"

"Didn't you hear his speech?"

"No, why?"

"He announced he's running for mayor."

"Oh."

"You know what else?"

"What?"

"Annie's got a new boyfriend."

"Huh?"

"Yeah, didn't you see them? They're right up there. He just moved here from New Mexico or Colorado or somewhere."

"I saw her. I didn't know she was with anybody."

"Wow, look at that one." Cates pointed up.

A big skyrocket went off just then, filling the sky with red and green streamers, and before the red and green had burned out a second pop came and a new flower of white burst in the sky. The crowd applauded joyously.

"Good one."

"Yeah."

"Listen, Frank, you wanna go to Mexicali tomorrow night?"

"Mexicali?"

"Uh-huh."

"How come?"

"How come? Are you kidding me? Not how come, but who come. We're gonna go to the bars. Come on, it'll be a blast."

"Who's going?"

"Me and you. And Shreve and Richard."

"You ask them yet?"

"Sure. I seen 'em earlier. They're all set. We'll go in my car."

"I don't know."

"Come on, why not?"

"I decided to take that job out in the desert."

"What's that got to do with anything?"

"I don't know."

"When do you start?"

"A week or so, maybe."

"A week. Cripes, man, I'm talking tomorrow night."

"Shoot." Frank laughed at his own weak argument.

"Shoot." Cates aped, punching Frank on the shoulder.

"Cut it out."

"Na, na, na. So, you coming or what?"

Frank didn't answer right away. He watched the fireworks with renewed interest. The fire department was lighting the last ones, a big ground level display of spinning wheels and a sparkling red, white, and blue flag. The field lit up well and he searched the crowd for Annie and her new boyfriend.

He saw them up ahead, holding hands and leaning against each other. He looked back at the burning flag and thought of the upcoming, isolated job in the desert. That thought somehow slipped into an image of Karen Edwards watering plants on her front porch.

"You broke a couple of big ones on this old field, didn't you, buddy?" Cates put his hand on Frank's shoulder.

"I guess I did." He remembered the previous fall and a long punt he'd returned homecoming night. "Okay, man, I'll go to Mexicali with you all."

"Great. I'll pick you up after work."

"Okay."

"Hot damn." Cates cheered. "Look out Mexicali, here we come."

23

SHREVE FELT LIKE HELL MOST of the morning—up one row and down the next—his head pounding to each belching chug of the tractor motor. At the end of each row, the same routine—raise the plows with the hydraulic lift, bang down the loose lift shaft on the left side with an eighteen-inch crescent wrench carried for that sole purpose, turn the tractor around, drop the plows, and head back down another set of rows, releasing an ammonia-laden cultivating mix into the growing cotton. Over and over, hour after hour, he worked right up to lunch time, which consisted of two salami sandwiches and a big soda pop, all of it too warm to really taste all that good, and taken under the sparse shade of a lone Tamarack tree at the south side of the field.

Finally, by early afternoon, with most of his hangover baked off by the sun and the cultivating mix running low on ammonia, he headed to the far southeast side of the field to the ammonia and butane tanks. Filling the ammonia, he nearly got down wind but tired as he was, leapt back to avoid the knockout potency of the ammonia gas. He'd forgotten once and damned near lost consciousness before he flung himself on the ground and crawled out from underneath the powerful, invisible strength of the ammonia. It was a lesson you only had to learn once.

Ducking behind the tank, he walked over to a wood trailer and drank two cups of water he poured from a rusty aluminum cooler. He knelt down, took off his crumpled straw hat and let a stream of cool water run over his sweat-matted hair. Wiping his hair back, he looked around and realized he was only a hundred yards or so of dirt and mown grass from Jeff and Marcie Clayborn's screened in back porch. To his surprise, he saw her two-thirds of the way across that flat space, walking his way. He leaned against the trailer and watched her coming directly toward him, dressed in clean, white shorts and a light blue T-shirt.

"Thought you could use one of these." She came right up to him and held out an ice cold Coors, which he gladly took.

"Thanks."

She watched him take a big guzzle of the beer. "Take it easy. There's more where these came from."

"It's hotter'n hell out here today."

"Hotter'n Mexico?" She winked.

"How'd you know about that?"

"This is Cotton, honey, everybody knows everything about everybody."

He nodded and took another drink of beer. Out of the corner of his eye he saw her checking him out. He lowered the beer and returned the favor. She looked beautiful. Her skin was tanned a perfect bronze. Her arms and legs were athletic and supple. Her breasts round and full, appealingly filling her T-shirt. She wore no makeup—at least none that the unskilled eye of a man could detect. And when she smiled, the recipient of that smile felt for the moment that he was the center of some lush and promising world. She was always cool. It was her essence. She radiated it.

"Get an eyeful, buster?"

"You always look so cool."

"Thanks, sugar, but if you keep me standing here much longer I'm afraid I'll just melt right down."

"That could never happen."

"Well, I don't want to find out." She rested an arm on his shoulder. They looked into each other's eyes but neither moved. "You want to get out of this sun for a while?"

"Is that an invitation?"

"Unless you're deaf and dumb, it was, sweetie."

"You call your husband 'darling' and 'sweetie'?" He set the empty beer beside the water can on the wood trailer.

"Baby, I don't call my husband at all."

He took her hands in his. There was only one other thing he wanted to know.

"He's gone to Brawley." She anticipated the question. "He always eats supper over at the Rancher's Club on Saturday nights. Then he goes to see one of his little floozies. We've got all the time we need."

She put her arm around his waist and slid her hand into his back pocket.

"Nice and firm." They walked toward the house.

"You're a straight shooter, aren't you?"

"None straighter."

"I like that in a woman." He put his arm around her. "I really do."

"Then we'll get along just fine."

Taking her hand out of his pocket, she took his hand in hers and led him into the cool comfort of her big, empty, ranch style house.

24

FRANK SUDDENLY STOPPED AND WORKED the bolt on his .22 rifle. He drew aim on a fat ground squirrel that stood to survey the sandy terrain outside its burrow. The rifle cracked and dust flew. The bullet zinged across the long-shadowed desert floor, sending the frightened ground squirrel scurrying into his hole. He popped the five-shot clip out of the .22 and reloaded it for the third time.

It was late afternoon and cooling, his favorite part of the day, especially since he had taken the job on Buck Clayborn's farm several miles outside Northland. The two *braceros* who helped Frank during the day had gone home and he relaxed from another ten-hour day of pulling out cherry tomato stakes and tending to a small fruit orchard across from his trailer.

After wasting another clip on the elusive ground squirrel, he began to walk back toward the trailer. He padded along outside the field, empty now except for the small wooden stakes the tomato vines grew on during season. About a quarter of the way back, he headed over to an abandoned silver trailer sitting off to one side of the field. He liked to sneak up on the rusty, unused trailer, and half for fun and half out of the paranoia living alone so far out of town engendered in him, he would burst into the trailer, rifle blazing like soldiers he'd seen fighting house to house in World War II films.

"*Yieee.*" He kicked the door open and crashed into the trailer. His first rounds, as usual, blasted into and through the flimsy, bullet-riddled back wall of the always-empty trailer. "Got you, you sons a guns," he cried at the invisible enemy.

He emptied the clip, firing the last four shots in four different directions. Smoke curled from the end of the barrel and floated in the stale air. He reloaded the clip and went back outside. The sun had set and dust hung low over the valley like a dirty brown fog. He headed for the trailer.

After washing up, he had his usual meal of two bologna and cheese sandwiches and a big Coke. As much as he enjoyed the late afternoon, he detested the coming of the black, dead-still night. He turned on all the lights in the trailer and picked up a *Life* magazine. Plopping in a chair by his bed, he reached over and switched on the radio.

Each night at the trailer was like the one before. He read magazines and listened to the radio, frequently getting up to check outside for signs of visitors, welcome or otherwise, until about nine when he got tired enough to try to sleep. The alarm was set for four-thirty so he had to get to bed early or he'd be worn out the next day.

Trying to sleep and doing it, however, were two different things. He lay in bed each night, loaded rifle by his side, his thoughts and imagination and the oppressive quiet of the desert combining to produce a level of anxiety that lasted until exhaustion allowed him to drift off to sleep.

Foolish fears of vampires, wild animals, and people sneaking up on him in the dark plagued him even though he was completely alone and well outside Northland. A rational person might realize this was probably one of the safest places in the entire world. But his superstitious nature and preoccupation with death conspired to leave him feeling vulnerable and isolated.

He felt trapped by the blackness of night, by the overwhelming mystery of existence, by the bone-chilling emptiness of a life in which we were born apparently without choice and from which we could leave only as a dead, conscious-less thing destined for worm food.

At these times he wished he could still believe in God, still find comfort in the belief of a hereafter, but logic and his own refusal to compromise denied him this option.

Lying in the dark, looking out the window, he saw stars twinkling in the clear night sky. He remembered his last spring back home in Jefferson, Arkansas before he and his mother moved to Cotton, when he had looked up at the star-filled sky and heard in their distant, icy stillness the answers to the questions troubling his adolescent mind. The answers were no, no, nothing at all. He came home late that night and different, for all time.

Now, well over two years later, lying in his rumpled bed with his hand on the .22, he began to drift off. He could only think about that stuff for so long. Eventually even fear wore off. He became used to it. It lost its edge. He forgot that he was afraid and went on living anyway.

Eyes blinking in the last moments before sleep, he saw himself wavering in the middle of an emotional road between abject fear of death and arrogant denial of God and faith. He sighed and rolled over in bed. When he opened his eyes again, it was four-thirty and the alarm was ringing loudly on the headboard behind him. He felt like he had not slept a single second.

25

FRANK HAD JUST EMPTIED A clip of .22 rounds into the deserted trailer and started back home when he saw the trail of dust billowing up behind a truck roaring down the road. Shreve. When he spotted Frank he started honking his horn and waving. Frank lifted the .22 in salute. Shreve skidded up in front of the trailer, dust rolling over the front of his pickup. He hopped out and walked up smiling.

"What the hell was all that shooting?" He held out a beer from a six-pack he carried. Frank took one, ripped off the pop-top and took a quick slug.

"Well, what was you blasting at? Coyotes?"

"Naw, just shooting."

"Sounded like a war." Frank looked around at the field and took another drink of beer. "I drive all the way out here to see you, and you clam up like a rock. What you been up to? Working hard or hardly working?"

"Working mostly. How 'bout you?"

"I'm still driving tractor for old King, or really Jeff Clayborn. It's an okay job."

"Are you not gonna go to VJC? For sure?"

"I don't think so, Frankie." They walked back towards Shreve's truck. He let the tailgate down and they sat on that, looking out at the orchard and the big canal a quarter mile beyond. "I'm making a good salary, I don't see any point to it."

"I always thought you'd go, at least to play ball."

"Nah. It's fun and all, but it'd be over in a couple of years. Might as well get a head start on work. Seems like old King likes me for some reason."

"All I'd want to do is play ball if I could."

"Yeah, but you're smart, you should go on to school. That's the right thing for you."

"I don't know about that." Frank looked at his dusty boots. He took off his dirty old straw hat and smoothed his hair back.

"Listen, buddy, VJC's fine for a year or so, but this valley's not for you. I expect you'll be going on to bigger and better things."

"You think so?"

"Sure."

"You, too."

"No, not me. This is my place." He indicated the wide expanse of the valley with a sweep of his arm. "This is where I belong."

Frank looked out across the valley. It stretched as far as the eye could see, to the Salton Sea and on, to the mountains above Palm Springs far in the distance. He breathed in the clean air, filled as it was with the dreams and hopes of a future that stretched as far as his mind's eye could see.

"Damn." Shreve slapped his leg, "I nearly forgot. You know that colored preacher lived up by you and your mom?"

"You mean Reverend Wilcox?"

"Yeah, that's his name."

"What about him?"

"He skipped out of town. Just up and took off."

"Up and took off?"

"Uh-huh. They're saying he ran off with all his church's money."

"You gotta be kidding." Frank remembered the burly man who showed up the day before the Fourth grilling him about Reverend Wilcox. There had to be a connection. "I wonder?"

"You wonder what?"

"Nothing. Just hard to believe he could do something like that."

"Well, I didn't know him myself, but I suppose if the dough was right—you know."

"I reckon."

"Some of the money he took he'd just got from that ladies group. The one Marcie Cotton's in."

"Marcie Cotton? How do you know what group she's in?"

"All the rich ladies of the valley, or at least the north end, are in it."

"Oh." It seemed like Shreve might want to say something else, but held back for some reason. "Marcie sure is pretty, ain't she?"

"She sure is, she's about the. . . ."

Shreve stopped and looked away. Frank studied the side of his friend's face. There was definitely something he wasn't telling.

"Something else happen?"

"I'll have to tell you some other time, pal. Let's have another beer. It's going to be a great sunset."

In the time he'd known Shreve, Frank never knew him to be so evasive about anything. Whatever this was.

"Sure, let's have another one."

26

KING COTTON SPENT THE MORNING driving around his many fields scattered throughout the north end. Among his vast holdings, he owned close to twenty-four hundred acres of his namesake plant in one hundred and sixty acre plots outside Cotton and Northland. But seeing these sweeping fields of green plants had not given him the pleasure they usually did. In fact, just the opposite.

A closer inspection revealed spotty growth in some of the fields, and in general the plants were not growing as well as in other years. King concluded they were not getting the irrigating they needed and that made him really mad. After stopping off at Galvan's for a heartburn-producing roast beef sandwich special, he climbed into his pickup and headed for the Valley Irrigation Commission in Imperial.

King hated dealing with the Commission. He had been one of its original founders, joining in loose affiliation with a small group of the biggest farmers in the valley to create the Commission in the late forties. But now almost all of those men were dead or retired, and the Commission had become a quasi-governmental agency run by career bureaucrats. King didn't like them, and they didn't like him.

"Maybe your irrigators simply aren't doing a good enough job, Mr. Cotton," a lumpy assistant superintendent suggested. He was the third of his kind King had been shuffled off to. The old man was at the edge of his low boiling point.

"Bullshit, it's not my men causing the problem."

"It's been a dry year, sir, that can adversely affect the crop."

"How long you lived around here, sonny?"

"Now, Mr. Cotton."

"Every damn year is a dry year in the valley. I was born out here when the Salton Sea was an empty salt basin and I've lived here ever since. There ain't been a half-dozen not dry years in all that time. So don't tell me about it being a dry year. Why do you think we made this Commission anyway?"

"Mr. Cotton, I appreciate your personal history and your part in starting the Commission, but the fact of the matter is there's just so much water to go around. There are more farms now than before, more requests for water. It's just the way it is."

"That's a bunch of crap. There ain't enough water getting up to the north end. And that's a fact."

"Mr. Cotton, what can I do? What do you want from us?"

"I want water, damn it. If my crop don't come in good because I don't get enough water, there'll be hell to pay. You remember that."

"Threats are not going to help, sir."

"Understand one thing, buddy, that ain't a threat, it's a promise. And you can tell your boss that for me, too."

King abruptly turned and stomped away. The Commission office was silent except for the sound of his big boots pounding the tile floor. He stopped at the door before going out.

"I better have all the water I need." He wagged his finger at the assistant superintendent. "Make sure it happens."

Out in his truck, King belched several times and tried to rub the burning tightness out of his chest. By the time he'd driven two or three miles toward Brawley, his chest hurt so much he had to pull off onto the side of the road. He took short, shallow breaths and tried to calm himself.

He thought about his children and how much he loved them. He thought about his wife, not as she was dying pitifully at the end, but in her prime, when she was nearly as lovely as the daughter they'd produced. Old or not, he didn't want to die yet, and he silently cursed the natural processes that robbed him of his robust body and left this worn out one in its place.

After a few moments, his breath got deeper, more regular. The pain subsided. He relaxed, purged his mind of the Commission and of farming. With a deep, tired sigh, he slowly pulled back onto the highway and headed home.

27

CATES AIMED HIS DAD'S .22 Magnum Ruger six-shooter at a slow moving coot swimming by a patch of tall bushes down in the muddy, water-filled canal beyond the farm where Frank worked.

"I can't believe Shreve beat me out here with all the news." He fired and missed the bird by ten feet. "Damn, just missed." The coot flew back up the canal out of harm's way.

"Right."

Frank sat on a rock behind Cates, sipping on a lukewarm Coors, his rifle leaning up against his leg. He finished the beer and pitched the empty can into the canal. Cates immediately fired two shots at it. He missed. Frank lifted his rifle, sighted and fired. The can skipped across the water.

"Got it."

"Easy with a rifle."

"I know."

"Hand me another beer, will you?" Cates reloaded the pistol.

Frank reached another lukewarm can out of the paper bag Cates brought.

"Here you go."

"Thanks." Cates popped the top and tossed it into the canal. "I bet Shreve didn't tell you who's coming to the fair, did he?

"No."

"Guess who?"

"I don't know."

"Come on."

"Buck Owens?"

"Buck Owens? Get serious. Why would he come to the county fair?"

"Why would anybody?"

Frank opened another beer and waited for Cates to tell him who was supposedly coming to the fair.

"Dion and the Belmonts."

"Dion and the Belmonts? Really?"

"Really."

"Wow, they're bigger'n Buck Owens, and they're coming? Wow! I can't hardly believe it."

"You never believe me."

"No, no, I believe you. It's just really big news, that's all. Dion and the Belmonts. Who would imagine them coming to our fair. I didn't know they played at fairs."

"Maybe there's a lot of stuff you don't know. Just because you think you're smart don't mean you know everything. You and Richard are just alike that way."

"I'm not smart. For sure not like Richard. I don't know a lot about anything."

"Right."

"No, really. A lot of times I don't know why I feel the way I do about something, or why I say certain things—usually at the wrong time. I don't understand other people. Why they do and say things. Sometimes it all seems real simple like there's nothing behind it, but at other times I can't figure nothing out."

"You know what your problem is? You think too much. And you take everything too serious. You stew about shit. Just do stuff and don't try to figure it out."

"Don't you want to understand what's going on in your life?"

"You got too much going on upstairs, Frankie. You gotta learn to shut it off ever' now and then."

Frank thought about that for a while. Cates might like to make up stories and act like a fool most of the time, but sometimes he was darned sharp. What he said made sense.

"That's good, Jimmy, you're right. Maybe I'll have to try that."

"Terrific." Cates blasted wildly at more coots in the canal. "Now try this one on."

"What?"

"What do you say we go to the revival at Northland Community Church this weekend."

"You gotta be kidding. I can't go there anymore."

"Sure you can. Reverend Kincaid will welcome you with open arms. The lost sheep and all that."

"Baloney."

"Okay, but there'll be lots of girls there. Karen Edwards, for example."

"I don't know."

"Sure, sure, it'll be overflowing with girls. We gotta go."

"Gotta go?"

"Absolutely." Cates walked to the edge of the canal to fire at more unsuspecting coots.

He fired twice, missed, and a coot took off down the canal to their right. Without hesitating, Frank swung his rifle up and away and fired. The coot fell like a rock into the canal. Cates spun around.

"Jesus," he exclaimed, "what a shot. How in the hell did you do that?"

"I don't know. I just shot at him. I wasn't thinking of nothing."

"Whew." Cates whistled. "Son of a gun. What a shot. Man, you should think of nothing more often."

"Yeah. That's what I need all right. To think of nothing more often. That would really help me."

28

I T WAS A MISTAKE TO go to the revival. There weren't any girls there, certainly not Karen Edwards anyway. Frank had let Cates talk him into going and now Cates had skipped out. Some traveling preacher ranted and raved about the Holy Spirit while Frank looked for a way to follow his buddy's lead and get out himself.

Stumbling and tripping over the frowning faithful, he made it to a side aisle and hung back in a corner trying to be inconspicuous. The choir stood to the right of the preacher—the same choir in which Frank had belted out his nasal monotone sounds. He remembered his last days in the church, how he attended only to be with Annie Bishop.

He had begun his withdrawal from God and religion before he left Jefferson, but kept on attending church out of habit, out of a need to make friends, out of a residual wish to belong to a group. But one day in the choir he looked over at Annie, looking so angelic in her white robe, and realized she was the only reason he came. Being in church just to see her seemed indefensibly dishonest.

He left church that day determined not to return. And, he had been as good as his word, until tonight. Head down, annoyed with himself, he slipped out the front door of the church and ran directly into his old minister, Reverend Kincaid.

"Frank, Frank Mason? Is that you?"

"Uh, hi, Reverend Kincaid."

"We've missed you at services. We—the kids—talk about you all the time. It's been a while."

"Well, I, uh, uh, been working a lot of weekends."

"Who are you working for these days?"

"Buck Clayborn, out in the desert."

"His brother Jeff is one of our regulars, you know."

"I know."

"Well, you come back soon, now. You're a good boy and we miss you. Be sure to give my best to your mother."

After the reverend went inside, Frank stood on the porch for a moment feeling small and guilty. The church man was honest and sincere and truly wanted the best for Frank's soul, whatever that was. Yet he had rejected the reverend and all he stood for. Standing there in the weak light of the church's front porch, he wondered why he'd changed so much in the last few months.

He didn't know why he had started drinking, or treating people poorly, or doing "bad" things like he did with the bar women in Mexicali. He didn't know why he'd stopped being a "good boy." But he did know being good was too hard for him. He couldn't keep it up.

Maybe you just couldn't be good all your life. Maybe that was too much to expect of anybody. Nobody could nowadays. There was just too much stuff going on. He took a deep breath and exhaled.

Bad or not, he knew he could never be the same guy he was six months before. He'd passed some invisible barrier from which there was no going back. With a last look at the old church, he stepped off the porch into the dark. Head down, he strode purposefully in the general direction of Galvan's. He had to find Cates and get a ride out to the trailer.

29

ON A QUIET FRIDAY NIGHT, Lar Turner grew bored sitting by the four-way stop, so he decided to cruise the east side and see if he could roust out some drunks—Mexican, black, or otherwise. He crossed the tracks and made a pass through the migrant worker area. There were a few private parties going on and loud *Norteño* music blared out the windows of a flimsy little bar some enterprising soul hastily had erected for the *braceros*, but Lar kept moving.

To kill more time he drove back to the highway and went into Cotton's black neighborhood. He passed by the once vibrant church where Reverend Wilcox had preached but which now stood dark and empty. The whole Reverend Wilcox episode was highly amusing to him, and he allowed himself a big smile in recalling the scandalous disappearance of the black minister.

He took a turn down by the big cotton gin that would soon be working around the clock, spewing its smelly cotton dust and residue all over the rundown shacks in the black quarter. Turning down one of the dirty little side streets, he let out a low whistle when his headlights lit up the familiar figure of Sandra Glover walking along the side of the road. He pulled his cruiser up beside her.

"What do you say?" His rakish smile was lost on Sandra. She didn't look up, but kept walking toward the next corner. He stayed right beside her.

"Darling, you gotta learn to be nicer to the police when we're on official business here in colored town."

Sandra stopped walking. He stopped the car alongside her.

"What you want?"

"Why, sweet meat, I just want a little of what these ugly bucks over here are getting."

"You go to hell."

"Aren't we the uppity one?" Sandra walked on. He paralleled her. "Now I was just trying to be friendly with my colored neighbors and you go and get all high toned on me. Like your old Reverend Mr. Thief used to do."

Sandra kept on walking. Lar leaned out the window of the squad car and leered at her.

"Come on, girl, I'm just looking for some fun."

She stopped dead in her tracks. He braked beside her.

"Lar Turner, you get outta here and leave me alone. Get back uptown where you belong. Go bother your lily-white folk over there. Stay out of here and leave us alone. We don't need you around here."

"Why, you sure are a mouthy bitch, ain't you? All you coloreds done got out of your heads since that damn southern preacher was here with his big shot Martin Luther Coon talk."

"You shut up about Pastor Wilcox and Reverend King. You don't know nothing about it."

"You better watch what you say, chocolate drop, or I'll run you downtown. You wouldn't want that again now—or would you?"

She immediately stopped talking back. The argument had reached a barrier through which she did not wish to pass. Lar gave her a victorious smile and began pulling away.

"Bye-bye, sweetheart."

She didn't look at him and he drove on. He reached the intersection and slowly pulled through it. In the rear view mirror he saw Sandra crossing beneath the streetlight. She held up a hand with the middle finger extended.

"I do like a gal with spunk." He turned down the street where Yellow Millie ran a bar out of her ramshackle home. "I truly do."

30

CATES LEANED BACK IN THE booth at Galvan's. "Well, if Billy's not going to be in town anymore, I sure as heck wouldn't mind seeing if she'd go with me."

"I heard some talk about her and Lar." Shreve looked out the window at the highway. Things were quiet for a Friday night, even for Northland. He spoke into the glass, which reflected Wanda Pate and Frank Mason's mother Kate as the ladies worked behind the counter across the room.

"Lar, Schmar," Cates cracked, "she's too young for him."

"You never know about that." Shreve turned away from the window. Marcie Clayborn's big Olds pulled into Galvan's parking lot. "But you're right. She's okay. I wouldn't mind it myself sometimes."

"How come you never tried when we were in school?"

"Billy hadn't been gone long enough, I—"

"Oh, my God." Cates cut Shreve off. "Here comes Marcie Clayborn. Man, is she good-looking or what?"

"Settle down, sonny. She's all right."

"All right? All *right*? I'd give your left nut for her."

Cates watched Marcie look around the café, wave at Wanda and Kate and then head directly toward him and Shreve.

"Oh, shit, she's coming over here."

"So what?"

"She's King Cotton's daughter, for crying out loud, Jeff Clayborn's wife. What'll we do?"

"Buy her fries and a Coke?"

"Knock it off, Shreve, she's right here."

Cates leaned back as Marcie reached the booth and gave her a feeble, idiotic looking smile. Marcie winked at him.

"Why, hello, boys." She focused her attention on Shreve.

"Hello."

"H—hi."

"Mind if I join you for a minute?"

"It's a free country." Shreve looked directly into Marcie's soft green eyes.

"Uh—uh, sure, Mrs. Clayborn." Cates cocked an eyebrow at Shreve's attitude toward the north end's best-looking woman.

"Call me Marcie." She sat down beside Cates.

"Okay, Marcie." Shreve maintained eye contact with her.

"Sure, Mrs. Clayborn." Cates's idiotic smile reappeared.

"Relax, honey. I don't bite."

Shreve snickered. Marcie gave him a sharp look.

Cates again raised an eyebrow.

"Well, don't let me stop your conversation. You boys go on. What were you talking about? The fair? The weather? I'm sure it was fascinating."

"Sure. What was it we were discussing, James? Politics? Religion? No, let's see, it was, oh, yeah, whatever happened between you and that girl down in Mexicali?"

"Knock it off." Cates blushed deep red. "That's not funny. I never had no girl in Mexicali, jeez." Marcie gave Shreve a sharp look.

"I'm sorry, buddy. I was just goofing you."

Marcie nodded approvingly.

"Aw, shoot. It's okay."

"Good evening, Mrs. Clayborn." Kate arrived at the table to take her order.

"Marcie, Mrs. Mason, please call me Marcie. All my friends do."

"Thank you, Marcie, and mine call me Kate."

"Your poetry reading for our club was just wonderful, Kate. Your sister's, too."

"Jean's had two poems accepted by poetry journals this past month and I've had three."

"That's great."

"Way to go, Mrs. M."

"Thank you, James."

"Now if you can just do something about that half-witted boy of yours living out in the desert like a hermit." Shreve joked. "You'll have really succeeded."

"You stinker, Shreve. I heard you were the first one to visit my 'half-wit.'"

"Somebody had to check on him, Mrs. M., I know you're too busy." Marcie gave him an appreciative leg nudge under the table.

"I know he appreciated it." Kate turned to Marcie. "So, what can I get you? I guess that was why I came over here in the first place, wasn't it?"

"Just get me one of your big old ice-cold cherry Cokes to go, will you, Kate? I've gotta be running along."

When Kate was back behind the counter, Wanda came over and sidled up next to her.

"If I didn't know better, I'd swear they were an item." They both looked over at Shreve and Marcie.

"Wanda, you are awful."

"What can I say?"

"Don't say anything." Kate put a lid on the cherry Coke.

She took the drink to Marcie and went back to work. Marcie stood to leave. Shreve and Cates rose with her.

"Well, tomorrow's another Saturday, maybe I'll see you boys running around the valley somewhere."

"Maybe." Shreve didn't look at her.

"Goodbye, Mrs. Clayborn." Cates just couldn't bring himself to call a woman like that by her first name.

Without looking back, Marcie walked out the door.

"Boy." Cates whistled as they watched Marcie drive off. "Is she something or what?"

"If you say so."

"If I say so? For crying out loud, Shreve, that woman is built like a brick shit house and beautiful, too. You'd love to get in her drawers, boy. You can't tell me you wouldn't."

"Well, since you put it that way, I suppose I would."

Cates scratched his chin. Shreve was a hard read sometimes. As hard as Mason—and that was saying something.

31

LAR TURNER WAS A HOUSE away from Yellow Millie's when her front door opened disgorging a stream of smoky light, a blast of Mississippi Delta blues music, and a drunk, wobbly, slow-minded Raymond Lewis. He staggered blindly out into the road forcing the police car to a skidding halt just feet from his bony body.

He looked into the glare of the squad car's lights, mild surprise and fear mingled in his uncomprehending expression. Lar piled out of the police car, long billy club in hand. Raymond shielded his eyes with one hand against the light. From behind the light, Lar emerged, a dark silhouette framed in yellow.

"Damn it. Is that you, Raymond?"

"Who there?"

"You are drunker'n shit, ain't you, boy?"

"What you want? Who is that?"

Lar stepped fully into the light. He held the billy club by his side.

"Is that you, Mr. Lar?" Raymond revealed a gap toothed smile.

"I oughta teach you a lesson, you drunk ass coon." Lar lifted the club and pushed it against Raymond's chest, who tried to back up but instead tripped and half-lunged, half-fell into the cop. Lar shoved him away, slapping him with the club. Raymond swung his arms up to protect himself.

"Put your hands down."

"Don't you hit me no more, Mr. Lar." Raymond pleaded, flailing his arms in all directions. Lar swung his club back and hit the drunk flush on the side of the head. He howled.

"Shut up." Lar bellowed, exploding in a violent fit.

He hit the scrawny black man over and over, until he slumped at the side of the road moaning. Lar hung above him, puffing and sweating.

"Dumbass son of a bitch." He hissed, as doors and windows began to open in the neighborhood. "You shut up."

"What's going on out there?" A man's deep voice.

"It's the police." Lar edged toward the police car.

"Who's out there with him?"

"He done beat up poor ol' Raymond." A woman cried.

A murmur spread on the wind through the neighborhood, grew quickly to a near collective shout. Lar got back in the car and shut the door. People ran up to Raymond, others began pelting the police cruiser with rocks. Lar slammed the car in reverse, spun around, hit low, and took off back down the road the way he came. In the rear view mirror he saw people, mostly younger ones, chasing him through the dust and flying gravel. They were firing a hail of rocks and refuse at the fleeing vehicle.

"Crazy bastards." Lar screamed out the window as he slid around the corner and headed for the safety of the highway. "Damn fools."

32

FRANK AND CATES STROLLED THE bright midway of the Imperial County Fair checking out girls and munching on cotton candy.

"Here you go, Frankie." Cates aimed them toward a booth where you threw softballs at a pyramid of metal milk bottles. "This is right up your alley. You're bound to win this one."

"I don't know."

"Come on, it'll be fun. It's only a quarter for three balls."

In the middle of Frank's second unsuccessful attempt at knocking the bottles down, a couple of cute girls wearing the red and white colors of Imperial High stopped to watch. Cates seized the opportunity.

"Throws good, huh?"

"Yeah." The smallest and cutest of the girls was fair-haired and thin, her partner, heavier and darker. The bigger girl's best features were a sweet smile and long, almost black hair.

"Well, he should be," Cates exaggerated. "He was All-Valley shortstop, two years running."

"Really? That's neat."

Frank paused with the last ball in his hand and turned around. Seeing the girls immediately flustered him. He turned back around to the game.

"Honorable Mention All-Conference," he mumbled, "one year."

"You were robbed, Frank." Cates gave Frank a 'don't-blow-it' slug to the shoulder. "You should've been First Team."

Frank fired the last ball at the two remaining bottles but it hit short and bounced up, only nicking the top of one bottle. He turned around sheepishly. The girls smiled.

"I didn't do too well there."

"Try it again." Cates pointed at the girls. They giggled.

"Sure, fellow, try it again." The oily carny stepped to the counter at the sound of easy business coming his way. "All it takes is two bits. One little old quarter. Three balls to win. Win a teddy bear for your sweetheart there." The girls giggled again. "Step on up and take another shot at her, pal. You can't lose. Not a big baseball star like you."

The carny dramatically rolled up a sleeve revealing a cheap tattoo of a big anchor with the letters "U.S.N." below it.

"Okay." Frank plopped a quarter in the carny's moist palm. The man handed him three lumpy softballs.

"Blast 'em, Frankie." Cates gave the girls another confident, knowing smile. The girls watched Frank intently. He cut loose at the bottles with three hard, accurate throws. One bottle remained standing.

"Good grief," Cates groused. "You couldn't have thrown better'n that. What's the deal? What are them things made of?"

"It's just what you see, buddy. Maybe your pal here just ain't strong enough to do the job."

"Baloney." The girls and Frank were to one side, out of the argument. He looked over at the little cute girl. She was looking at him. "He's got the most accurate arm in the valley."

"If he's so good, let him try again. Put your money where your mouth is."

"What do you say?" Cates turned to Frank. "You can do it, right?"

"I don't know, Jimmy."

"Sure you can." The dark-haired girl pumped him up. "You're good. You almost knocked them all down the last time."

"Do it or move on." The carny acted disinterested.

He leaned against the counter and leered at the girls. Frank dug in his jeans but only found a dime. He had a couple of bucks left, but didn't want to bring them out and show the girls how little money he really had.

"I only got a dime left. I don't want to break a bill."

"I got change, sonny. It's the idea."

"Here." Cates pulled a quarter out of his pocket. "Do it."

The carny handed Frank three balls, set up the milk bottles and backed out of the way.

"All yours, Pee Wee."

Frank wound up and fired the first ball, knocking the top bottles off. Cates and the girls cheered. The carny pulled out a toothpick and began chewing on it. Frank's second throw knocked over one of the bottles on the ground.

"Come on, Mason. You got this. You can do it."

Frank reared back and fired a direct hit into the last two bottles. One fell, the other barely budged.

"Hey!" Cates slammed his fist down on the wooden counter. "That was perfect. That should've knocked 'em all down."

"No way. That last ball was crap."

"It hit right in the middle of them."

"So what? What are you saying?"

"We're saying we should've won."

"Yeah." The dark-haired girl agreed.

"You saying I'm cheating, boy?" The red-faced, frowning carny squared up aggressively.

"I'm saying that last ball hit right smack in the middle and them bottles should've fell over."

The carny advanced as if he were going to leap over the counter and attack. Frank pulled Cates away. The girls stepped back.

"Skip it, forget it. It's just a stupid game. We only lost a buck or so."

"Well, it's a bunch of baloney." Cates called over his shoulder as Frank tried to lead him away.

"Get outta here." The carny called after.

"Yeah, yeah, yeah." Cates got his arm loose and settled down. "What happened to the girls?"

They stopped and looked back. The girls were already making their way down the midway in the other direction. They watched as two other guys came up and started talking to the girls. The little cute one looked back at them.

"Well, darn it. Wouldn't you know it, Mason, we blew it again."

"I guess so."

"Ah, what the heck." Cates dipped into his seemingly bottomless reservoir of optimism. "There's plenty of fish in this sea." He indicated the packed fairgrounds with the sweep of an arm.

"Sure. Sure there is. There's plenty of fish in the sea."

33

T HE ANTELOPE VALLEY BOYS?" FRANK looked at the big sign in front of the auditorium where the fair's musical shows were held. "Seriously? Cates, what happened to Dion and the Belmonts?"

"Hey, so maybe they couldn't make it. I was wrong. So what?"

"So I ain't going in there. I ain't paying for that."

"Nobody's making you."

"Lucky for you Shreve ain't here. He'd ride you out of the county."

"Big deal. It coulda happened."

"What could've happened?" A girl's voice from behind Frank and Cates. They turned around to see who it belonged to.

"Annie." Frank couldn't hide his surprise.

"Hey, kiddo. What's up?"

"You guys going in?"

"Nah, Mason's feeling sorry for himself 'cause Dion and the Belmonts didn't show."

"Liar."

"Dion and the Belmonts? Who said they were coming?"

"Mason." Cates lied.

"Did not."

"Where's the new guy?"

"Getting us some treats." Annie turned to Frank. "How's your mom?"

"Fine."

"I hear you all went to Mexico." Cates chuckled. Frank let out a loud breath.

The new boyfriend appeared with a couple of hot dogs and Cokes. He was an average guy, about as big as Cates, but a little thick in the waist and hips. He had sandy, curly hair and thick eyebrows, an insincere smile, and a questioning look for the two boys.

"What's up?" He handed a hot dog and Coke to Annie. His right hand was adorned with two big, ridged rings.

"Oh, David, this is Jimmy Cates and Frank Mason from Cotton. They just graduated. This is David Lane. He's from New Mexico."

"Mason, huh?" Lane lifted a bushy eyebrow. "I heard of you."

"You going to Cotton next year?" Frank tried to be polite.

"Cotton? That little dump? Hell, no, I been out of school a year already. No more kiddie crap for me." Frank and Cates exchanged glances.

"Jimmy and Frank are going to Valley this fall. You start this week, don't you, guys?"

"We register and stuff," Frank said. Cates was quiet. He looked ticked off.

"I seen that place," Lane cracked, "not much of a college. A couple of outhouses in the middle of nowhere."

"David, be nice."

"It's as good a school as any cactus JC you got in New Mexico." Cates was having none of the new guy's attitude.

"That's funny. How would you hayseeds know a good school anyway, probably can't even read."

"You know what, pal?" Cates pointed at Lane, who pushed his hand away.

"What?"

"You're a real butthole."

"You're an asshole, hick."

Annie tried to get in between them as a small crowd gathered around. Lane pushed Cates in the chest. Cates returned the favor, knocking Lane's hot dog and Coke to the ground. Lane swung at Cates, hitting him in the shoulder and knocking him backwards.

"Stop it," Annie yelled. "Frank, stop them."

Frank moved forward, but Cates had recovered and lunged towards Lane. They grappled, slinging each other around. Frank waded in, goaded by Annie and against his better judgment. What he got was a deflected right hand from Lane that landed high on his cheek, the two ridged rings scraping underneath his eye.

"Ow."

"Keep out of it." Lane yelled.

He and Cates circled each other a couple of times, fists held up like old bare knuckle fighters. Annie stood to one side crying. Frank put a hand to his skinned up cheek. A burly security guard burst out of the crowd and in between the scuffling boys.

"That's enough of that. You boys knock it off or I'll boot the both of you out of here."

"I'll see you again." Lane spoke over the guard's shoulder.

"Screw you." Cates growled.

"You and your mother."

Cates lunged at Lane, but the guard held him back.

"Make another move, and I toss you."

He and an embarrassed Annie walked away. The guard held Cates.

"Let go. They're gone."

"You settled down?"

"Yeah, yeah, I'm okay." The guard released him.

"You boys just ride a ride or play some games and stay out of trouble now, you hear?"

"Yes, sir." Frank rubbed his cheek.

"See that you do." The guard headed down the midway in the same direction Annie and Lane had gone. Cates and Frank took off the other way.

"Is that guy a jerk or what, huh, Frank?"

"Man, I'd say. What a jerk."

"Boy, Annie deserves better'n that spaz."

"She sure does."

"To hell with that useless piece of crap. Him or no stupid carny's gonna foul up my fun. Let's go ride the Tilt-a-Whirl. What do you say?"

"Sounds good."

"Maybe we'll run into those Imperial girls again."

"Sure, Jim, sure. We might."

34

LOOK AT THAT BABY DIVE." Cates pointed his can of soda off toward the Chocolate Mountains. Frank searched the sky for signs of a jet. He picked it up just as it dropped below the brown peaks of the distant range. The plane immediately arced back up into the sky. A moment later two puffs of smoke appeared on the far desert floor.

From their vantage point on top of a tall dune in the sand hills that stretched from just outside Cotton almost to Yuma, the boys watched the jets from the El Centro Naval Air Station bombard the barren terrain leading to the Chocolates. Behind them, in the shade at the bottom of the dune, Frank's Uncle Carl Waters slept in his Jeep, resting after a couple of hours of riding in the dunes and more than a couple of cooler-chilled Coors.

"It ever occur to you, Mason, that all we ever do is come out here to this godforsaken desert? Ever notice that?"

"Everywhere's the desert out here."

Frank sipped his own soda and felt the scab on his cheekbone where he'd taken the glancing blow from David Lane's twin-ringed right hand during the recent altercation at the Imperial County Fair.

"You know what I mean."

"But the dunes are really great." Frank looked around at the soft hills of sand stretching southeasterly as far as one could see. "Beats the heck out of working at Buck Clayborn's like I was. That was too far out. This is a good place here."

"For lizards and horny toads."

"Well."

"That's us all right." Cates walked several feet away, across the top of the dune.

Alone for the moment, Frank closed his eyes, listening to the light wind coursing over the sand hills and to the silence of the land beyond. When he opened his eyes again he concentrated on the Chocolate Mountains. They were so sharp and clear against the horizon it was as if he could reach out and touch them.

For that flash of time he felt content, almost happy. He saw and felt, briefly, an interdependency of sun, air, and land. A wave of tranquility swept over him and he felt in a sudden rush the symmetry of nature, the hope of the future, the sense that somehow everything was all right. Cates' voice slowly brought him back to the real world.

"I said I seen Carol Scott with old Lar the other day."

"With Lar? What about Billy Cotton?"

"He's been gone a long time now."

"Hmm." Frank rubbed his chin. "I always figured it would be Shreve if Billy C. never came back."

"I kinda like her myself." Cates gave Frank a sideways look.

"You do?"

"Yeah, I even asked her out."

"You're kidding."

"No."

"When?"

"Before the fair."

"Well, I'll be. What did she say?"

"I don't know. She kinda didn't really say yes or no. Then I seen her with Lar and I figured she wasn't interested."

"You should try again. She's real pretty."

"How come you don't ask Karen Edwards out?"

"Oh, no, I couldn't do that."

"Why not?"

"I don't know how to do that stuff."

"You managed to talk Terri Mangrum into going to the Senior Dance with you."

"That was different. I had to go with someone."

"You still did it."

"Yeah, I guess I did."

"Speaking of doing it." Cates picked up a small rock and tossed it across the dunes. "Did I tell you about Marcie Clayborn coming up and sitting with me and Shreve up at Galvan's?"

"No, when?" Frank finished his soda and shook out the last drops onto the dunes. They made little round dark stains in the sand. "What did she do?"

"It was right before the fair. We were just sitting there BS'n and she came right in and plopped down with us. Sat next to me."

"You're kidding."

"Huh-uh. Your mom saw. She was working that night."

"So what happened?"

"We just talked. But I think maybe her and Shreve got something going."

"Come on. No way."

"No, I'm serious. There was something about the way they looked at each other. She was really friendly."

"She's always really friendly. That's the way she is, that's all."

Frank flashed to Shreve visiting him out in the desert. It seemed like he had been about to reveal something, then stopped. And Marcie had told him to give Shreve a special hello for her that time she came by Buck Clayborn's.

"We better go wake up Uncle Carl. He's liable to burn up in the Jeep."

They slid down the dune, leaving long tracks in the soft, slippery sand.

"I think they're doing it." Cates reached the bottom of the dune first.

"It's still hard for me to believe."

"Maybe you're right."

"Maybe."

"Maybe you ain't."

"Yeah." Frank walked around to the driver's side of the Jeep. "That, too."

35

"TAKE THAT, SHRIMP." BIG STEVE Butler blasted an overhand slam across the table at Frank. In self-defense, he backhanded the ball and returned it, the ball ticking the side of the table and dropping to the ground, unhittable, for another point. "You lucky turd."

"Point-eighteen." Frank pointed his paddle at the 6-foot-2, 210 pound star VJC pitcher and basketball forward. Butler frowned and growled.

"Do it, shorty."

Frank made a solid serve that was returned in a high arc. A hard backhand slam with just enough English on it caused Butler to return the ball into the net.

"Shit. Lucky twerp."

"Game."

"Rematch." Butler headed off a short, nervous kid in glasses who had the next game but no desire to insist on that right with the big jock. "I got winner."

"I got class." Frank tossed his paddle down for the nervous kid to use. The kid eyed the paddle but didn't immediately pick it up.

"Class? Hell, Mason, you ain't done nothing but play whist, snooker, and ping pong since you got here. C'mon, play me again. Forget class."

"I gotta go. We got a test in Poli Sci."

"Chickenshit. I'll kick your butt tomorrow, boy." With a disgusted snort, Butler began his ping-pong assault on the nervous kid.

Frank grabbed his books and headed for class. He didn't have a test, but he did have to go to classes sometimes. There was more than a little truth in what Butler had said about him.

With a few minutes yet to spare, Frank leisurely strolled along between classroom buildings, breathing in the clean air and fantasizing about starring on the VJC baseball team next spring. An insistent female voice calling his name finally brought him back to reality just as he was rapping a solid line drive down the right field line for a sure double.

"Frank. Frank Mason."

"Hi, Sandra. How you doing?"

"Got a topic picked out for your paper yet?"

Frank saw another old Cotton High buddy, Tony Ruglia, hanging out with some other kids a couple of buildings away.

"Sort of."

"What's it about?"

"I was thinking of writing about the U.S. getting out of the United Nations."

"Get out of the U.N.? What would we want to do that for? The U.N.'s the best hope there is for world peace."

"Well, all we ever do is foot the bills for everybody else." Frank echoed what he'd heard from men like Buck Clayborn and Dale Honeycutt. "And then the Communists and those other little countries just shove it in our face."

"I don't know about that."

"What's yours on?"

"Police brutality."

"Police brutality? What does that mean? You mean when police are real rough on prisoners?"

"That's part of it. But it's more than that. It's any time the police use excess force against anybody. Prisoners or regular citizens."

"Does that happen much?" Frank squinted one eye. "I mean to people that ain't crooks."

"Plenty." They reached the political science building.

"Really? It's a real problem? For who? Where? That's hard to believe."

"It's not hard to believe if it's happened to you."

"Do you mean?"

"It's time for class." Sandra stepped ahead of him toward the door. "Maybe some other time."

"But—"

"We gotta go in." She hurried into the classroom leaving a puzzled Frank at the door.

He stood there for a moment trying to imagine what she had been getting at. She couldn't have meant what he thought she meant. That couldn't be, could it? With a shrug, he entered the classroom. Sandra had already taken a seat up front by some other kids. He took a chair in back and sat by himself.

36

YOU MAY HAVE THE OLD man buffaloed." Jeff Clayborn pointed at Shreve, who glared back at him. "But I ain't buying in to your crap, boy."

A couple of Mexican irrigators, who understood Jeff's tone but not most of his words, stood to one side with David Lane. Lane was newly hired by Jeff and had been put on the crew over Shreve's objections. Lane and the irrigators pretended they weren't interested in the developing argument between the two bosses.

"I don't know what you're doing just yet, but I'll guaran-damn-tee you I'm gonna find out."

Jeff glanced over at Lane, who rubbed his neck and coughed. The exchange wasn't lost on Shreve.

"You got something you accusing me of?"

"I'm saying it's funny that just the fields you're working on are growing good. No matter what's happening, you just got plain damn fool's luck to have the old man gulled like you do."

"You got something on me, Clayborn, take it to Mr. Cotton. Let him decide. He hired me, he give me ever' job I've had here so far. He can fire me, too. But he makes the call. Not you."

"That may change." Jeff's face was as red as his sunburned neck.

A couple of weeks back, when there was no more tractoring to be done on the crop, King had given Shreve his own crew, small as it might be, to take care of several fields of promising cotton and to prepare the equipment for the harvest. To repay King's trust in him, he had taken to diverting water and doing extra irrigating of those fields which were looking the best.

Overall, the cotton crop looked like it could be one of the worst in years and farmers all over the valley were scrambling to do whatever they could to improve the yield. It particularly galled Jeff that this upstart newcomer should be doing so well when experienced hands like himself were struggling.

"Well, you get these damned Mexicans to work. I've got to go to Brawley and I want to see 'em busting their humps when I get back. Understand me?"

"That's what we were getting ready to do."

"Stupid damn wetbacks." Jeff griped at his dusty cowboy boots on the way back to his pickup. "Smart ass, wet-behind the ears, know-it-all kids."

Shreve turned back to his crew. The irrigators busied themselves with shovels and chunks of hose. Lane gave him a nauseating, overly familiar ain't-life-a-bitch smile. Shreve briefly considered how enjoyable it would be to take out his annoyance with Jeff on this Lane character. He was a real pisser, this new guy.

"Boy." They watched Jeff pull away in a cloud of dust. "Boss sure was in a bad mood today. That's the way with the big bosses. They're kind of—temperamental. Yeah."

"He ain't the boss." Shreve's voice was as hard and emotionless as he could make it. "I am. Now get over there and help Cesar and Leon."

"Help them? They're Mexicans. I'm not supposed to be doing the irrigating. C'mon, man, be white about it."

"Get your butt over there."

"Aw, man."

"Do it."

"Hell, Jeff, uh, Mr. Clayborn, said I would be doing mechanic type stuff. Not this wetback crap."

"Mr. Clayborn ain't running this crew. I am. Now go help 'em or get the hell out."

"All right, all right. I'm going."

The two irrigators looked up and snickered.

"Shut up."

"*Besamé culo, cuñado.*"

"What the hell'd he say? I don't know Mexican."

"Cesar said you're okay, for a white man. Right, *cuñados?*" Cesar and Leon laughed some more.

Lane stomped over to them and started banging a shovel around.

"Kiss my ass, *cuñados.*" He aped the one word he'd understood.

"*Muy bien, hombre.*" Leon saluted. "*Muy bien.*"

"What'd I say?"

"You can think about it while you're irrigating this field. Let's go."

"Shit." Lane followed the irrigators to the edge of the field. "What a crap-ola deal this is."

Shreve headed towards the irrigation canal running alongside the head of the field nearest them. Jeff Clayborn and David Lane be damned, he was going to have the best fields in the north end even if he had to work day and night to do it and divert every drop of water in the whole damn valley in the process.

37

FRANK SMILED AS HE WALKED into the union. He could still hear the laughter from his description of the *Dying Gaul* as being a great sculpture because it was so "alive." What a dope. His comment, intended to impress the young lady professor, had cracked up his Humanities classmates and, then, even himself. It really was a dumb thing to say.

He looked around the cafeteria, spotted Tony Ruglia and Sandra Glover at a table in the middle of the room. Tony stood just as Frank pulled out a chair to sit down.

"Whoa. Don't leave 'cause I got here."

"I'm not." Tony collected his books from the table. "Unlike some of us, I have to attend class here at dear old VJC."

"Hey, I go to class. That's where I'm coming from."

"Sure, Mason, sure. I believe you."

"Get outta here."

"See you later."

"See you later, Tony."

"Is it okay if I sit here?" Frank slid his chair around to face Sandra as Tony walked away.

"Why, of course it is." He plopped his books down and sighed. "Tough class?"

"Oh, no, it was a fun one, really. We had a good time."

He looked around the union. He saw a few kids from some of his other classes, but nobody else from Cotton.

"So, how are you doing?"

"Okay. How 'bout you, Sandra?"

"Fine."

"You like it here at VJC?" He rubbed the back of his neck and looked down at the table. He wasn't sure if she wanted to talk or not.

"Uh-huh."

"Better'n CHS?"

"Maybe, or maybe it's just different. But I like it okay. How about you?"

"I think I like Cotton better. I knew all the kids. Used to it, I guess."

"Sometimes you can get too used to a place. Know it too well. And people can know you too well. Know too much about you. Or think they do."

"Sandra." Frank haltingly framed the question he'd wanted to run by her for weeks but had been too afraid. "Don't be mad at me, but did Reverend Wilcox really run off with all your church's money?"

"You're the first person I know who's even asked that question. Everybody else assumed he did it and that's that."

"Just wondering. He lived by me and my mom and he didn't seem like that kind of man."

"Who told you that he stole everything?"

"Aw, you know. Everybody."

"Everybody meaning Lar Turner?"

"Well, not *just* him."

"But mostly him?"

"There were other people saying it."

"Frank, I know you and your buddies are friends with Lar."

"Not exactly friends."

"There are things about Lar you white people don't know nothing about."

"What do you mean?"

"Things that wouldn't stand the light of day."

"Are you saying Lar is like the cops you described in your paper for Poli Sci about police brutality?"

Sandra looked around the union, then back at Frank.

"Yes."

He leaned back in his chair.

"But what about Reverend Wilcox? What happened to him?"

"We don't really know. It was so sudden no one knew for certain. The money disappeared and he left town, but I still don't believe for a minute he stole it."

"Me, neither. But we'll probably never know the complete truth, will we?"

"No. I guess we won't."

38

"HEY, MOM." FRANK CALLED INTO the kitchen from the living room. "I'm gonna take a walk. I'll be back in a little bit."

"Okay, son." His mother came to the open kitchen door. "If I'm not here when you get back, I'll be over at your Aunt Jean's. We're going to work on some poems tonight."

"Okay." He crossed the living room to the front door. "I'll see you later."

He left the apartment and took the stairs down to the sidewalk. Outside, a light breeze was blowing and it was still warm, but he could feel a hint of coolness in the air. The first sign of fall coming to the valley. He took a deep breath and walked by Manny Ruiz's market toward Cotton's city park. The sun was low in the sky and in his eyes, so he decided to take a longer walk around town and end up back at the park before going home.

He turned left off Main onto Church Street, away from the smaller north side of the city park that included the fire and police stations and the Little League field, and headed south down toward the community church and Annie Bishop's house. He crossed the big field in the park and walked slowly through its short, brown grass.

With most everyone inside getting ready for supper, he walked undisturbed. He strolled along giving free rein to his thoughts. He exited the south end of the field, only a half block from Annie's and memories of her welled up in his consciousness.

He recalled their first kiss. How he had been so nervous and clumsy and how she had been so sweet and patient. She was a decent girl and deserved better than he had given her and she for sure deserved better than this new guy David Lane.

He passed her house without looking over, lost in a fantasy of punching out Lane. At the end of the block, he turned right past Palm Street and then right again on Western, paralleling the outer fields of CHS. It was getting late now and the sun dipped below the horizon, its last rays mingling with the shadows to produce an atmosphere of tranquility and beauty matched, and perhaps slightly exceeded, only by those first few moments at sunrise. He ambled along, taking it all in, content for the time being to blend with the last shadows of the day, to fade into the dark of Cotton's imminent night.

Even though it was dusk, he followed an impulse and walked toward CHS instead of going straight back to the park. He tramped across the lot beside the football field and then crossed the track onto the burnt grass of the playing surface itself. Old memories of games he'd played on the field flooded his mind. He was so absorbed in his thoughts he didn't realize he had passed beneath the goal posts at the other end of the field until the sound of a slamming car door roused him to his surroundings.

In the weak light, he made out the car but had to lift his eyes to the horizon to be able to tell much about it. From the dark markings on the side, it appeared to be a Cotton police car and he thought it must be Lar but couldn't tell for sure. Walking on, he neared the vehicle when he realized there was more than one person in it. He stopped in his tracks. There was a woman's voice low and indistinct at first, then sharper and clearer. Then he heard Lar's voice, loud and angry.

"Get your damn pants off." The policeman ordered an unseen woman who seemed to be resisting, at least it seemed so from the scuffling sounds coming from the car.

Frank knelt down and held his breath. He didn't know whether to run or stay where he was. There was a moan and a grunt from the car, obviously Lar, and then a cry from the girl.

"Damn it."

Frank edged backwards, squat-legged, toward the football field. There was a lot of grunting and groaning in the car. Then the girl spoke. Her voice sounded sad, plaintive, familiar.

"Don't, Lar," Carol Scott entreated, "you're hurting me. Don't do it so hard."

Her plea was followed by what sounded like a slap and then she was quiet. Frank rose to a crouch and jogged to the football field, then ran back toward town as fast as he could go. He felt guilty—like a thief, or a sneak. He thought of the guys, Billy Cotton, Shreve, even Cates, who still might have an interest in her. That she should have chosen Lar Turner instead seemed unfathomable. She was a good-looking girl, better than Lar should have, way more than he deserved.

By the time he passed the fire station, now walking, it was completely dark and he was glad it was. He felt embarrassed by what he had stumbled onto and how he reacted to it. Instinctively he knew what other people did was none of his business unless it affected him directly, which this did not. But he could not easily shake off a strong sense of disappointment or disillusionment, generalized or unjustified though it might be. Painfully aware of his own lack of sophistication, he headed home in the dark feeling stupid and small. His pace was deliberate, and slow.

39

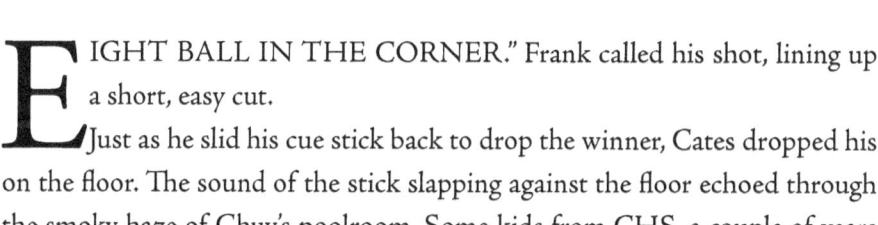

EIGHT BALL IN THE CORNER." Frank called his shot, lining up a short, easy cut.

Just as he slid his cue stick back to drop the winner, Cates dropped his on the floor. The sound of the stick slapping against the floor echoed through the smoky haze of Chuy's poolroom. Some kids from CHS, a couple of years younger, looked up from their table in front of the room. A third table, lit like the other two by a weak bulb hanging directly above it, was empty.

"Sorry."

"Thanks a lot. You better watch that, you know Frosty gets all pissed when we mess with the cues."

"Yeah, yeah."

Frosty was the racker at Chuy's, collecting a dime a rack—his sole income as far as any of the boys who frequented the pool hall knew. Teenage boys in the back of a pool room only separated from the bar by a flimsy partition already bordered on the edge of legality, so the boys knew anything short of tearing the place up would probably be ignored by Chuy and the feisty, but ineffectual Frosty. Frank sighted again and cleanly sank the eight ball.

"Game."

"Rack." Cates called to Frosty, who dozed in a chair in a dim back corner.

The old man got up slowly, mumbling an unintelligible complaint, and racked the table for another game of eight ball. Cates tossed him a dime. Frosty turned the coin over several times, then dropped it in a pocket of his dirty, baggy pants and went back to his chair.

"You break."

Frank leaned against the table, cue resting against his arm. He remembered another night when he and Richard Martin shot at the table where the CHS kids were now. Richard had stopped in mid-shot to start conjugating Spanish verbs for the edification of Gilbert Cruz. And then started singing "Mr. Bass Man" with such gusto that it caused old Frosty to get cantankerous and threaten to stop racking the tables until they "stopped making that goldarned racket." Frank laughed out loud.

"What's so funny?"

"I just remembered some funny stuff Richard did in here is all."

"We had some good times in this place, didn't we?"

Frank broke with a powerful stroke of the cue. The rack was good and the balls scattered around the table. The three ball fell.

"I got solids."

He sank the five in the side, six in the corner, before missing a cross side bank on the one.

"Good try."

"Seems like everybody's going their separate ways, now, don't it Jimmy?"

"Yeah." Cates sank the twelve ball in the side. "Richard's off to college and Shreve works all the time."

They exchanged a smile. They were convinced they knew what Shreve was working at these days. And it was a lot more than farming.

"But, hey. I'm still here."

"Not for long. You're going to work in El Centro." Frank frowned. Cates missed the eleven in the corner.

"That's life, pal. Times change. Life goes on. At least we'll still both be going to good old VJC."

"Right."

"Sides, you can keep busy watching 'em build the new four-lane."

"The new what?"

"Oh, yeah, it's gonna be great. They're putting in a four lane."

"A four lane? Where?"

"Here. The highway through town. It'll be like a freeway. All the way from Calexico to Indio. It's gonna change the whole valley, completely. Ain't it bitchin', man?"

"Where'd you hear that?"

"I heard it, around."

"The same place you heard all the other stuff, I bet. Like Nixon coming to Cotton. Or Dion at the fair."

"Hey, that stuff could've happened. It was just bad luck. Maybe they changed their minds, that's all."

Frank leaned against the table and belly laughed. Cates got tickled, too. Their noise rousted Frosty who came up grousing.

"You boys shoot pool or move on. I can't make a living off you standing there howling like a couple of sick coyotes."

Frank tried to line up a shot, but he was laughing too hard.

"Shoot." Cates cackled like a hen.

"Oh, heck." Frank shot the four ball at the corner, missing it by a good three inches. He and Cates howled. Frosty cursed a blue streak.

"Damn fool kids." The old man rubbed the gray stubble on his chin. "Crazier'n a bunch of loons."

40

SHREVE SAT IN HIS SWIM trunks in a lawn chair by the pool in Marcie's back yard drinking a beer and looking at the cotton fields stretching out across the valley. It was late afternoon, cooling and peaceful. He heard the back door open and close and the sound of her sandaled feet approaching. She came up behind and put a hand on his shoulder.

"Two *pesos* for your thoughts." She sat on the edge of a pool chair. She wore her bikini bottoms and Shreve's short-sleeved shirt, the top three buttons opened.

"Huh?"

"What'cha thinking about?"

"Oh, not much."

"I bet you were thinking about work."

He looked at her. She still looked beautiful, but for some reason he didn't understand, a small sense of distance had insinuated itself between them.

"Actually, I was thinking about this new butthole on my crew. From Arizona or New Mexico or somewhere."

She traced the outlines of his face with her eyes.

"What's his name?"

"Something Lane. Donald or David. Yeah, David, David Lane."

"Annie Bishop's new boyfriend."

"Annie Bishop and this guy are going together?"

"Didn't you know that?"

"I don't pay attention to that stuff."

"She was your friend's girlfriend before, right?"

"You mean Frank Mason?"

"Yes. What's he like?"

"Frank? He's a good guy. We played ball together. He's good with the books."

"Why did they break up?"

"How would I know? I mean, I don't keep track of other people's lives. I got enough to do worrying about my own."

"And you don't need me complicating it."

"I didn't say that."

"But you won't be needing me much longer."

"What do you mean by that?" They'd never had a conversation like this before. He didn't much like it.

"Darling. You have captured my daddy's eye. You're his new golden boy. He's already given you your own crew."

"Two *braceros* and a fathead loser ain't much of a crew."

"It still is one, though, and it's yours."

"That doesn't have anything to do with me and you."

"But it will. People will start to talk. They'll say you made it with Daddy because you were banging me."

"I am banging you." Shreve tried to joke.

"You know what I mean."

"No way." He reached over and took her hand. She didn't resist.

"You're going to be a big farmer someday, too. With your own ranch house and your little wifey and your beer belly and your Mexican or Filipino girlfriend for your fun."

"You got it all figured out, don't you?"

"I've been around it all my life, hon. That's how the story goes."

"Well, this story ain't done quite yet." He stood and gently pulled her toward him. She hooked a finger in the elastic of his trunks.

"Think you'll keep me for a while?"

"Wouldn't have it any other way, darling." He led her back into the house. She held onto his hand, and followed behind.

41

CATES AND FRANK WERE IN the middle of their fifth game of eight ball when Uncle Carl came wobbling in the back door of Chuy's. "Look, Mason."

"Hey, Uncle Carl."

"Hi, boys." He happily waddled towards them. "What you fellers doing?"

"Shooting some eight ball, Mr. Waters."

"Many's the time I played here myself."

"I didn't know you shot pool, Uncle Carl."

"Back during the war. I got fairly good."

"No kidding?"

"But you young fellers don't want to hear an old coot like me go on about the old days."

"Sure we do." Frank stretched the truth a bit.

If Uncle Carl decided to recite the Constitution right there in the pool hall, he was prepared to listen to every word rather than be rude or hurt his uncle's feelings. Carl saved him that altruistic sacrifice.

"I gotta go on in to Chuy's and get me a drink of water or something. Let me get you all a Coke."

"You don't have to do that."

"Sure, sure, I don't mind." Carl weaved off to the bar.

Some young guys at the next table snickered. Cates and Frank frowned at them, then went back to shooting pool. In a couple of minutes, Carl re-emerged with a soda in each hand. He distributed them and got a round of polite thanks in return.

"What you doing out tonight, Uncle Carl?"

"What's that?" Carl put a hand to his ear to hear better.

"What you up to?"

"Oh, Lord. Your mama and the old woman's at the house scribbling away and they done chased me out. Worked up a good thirst getting out of there, too."

"Well, we'll see you, Uncle Carl. Thanks for the Cokes."

"You take care of that thirst now, Mr. Waters."

"All right, boys." Carl went back to the dark bar beyond the partition.

"What a great old guy. He kills me."

"Yeah. He's a great uncle."

"You think he bought them Cokes so we wouldn't tell your Aunt Jean he was half-crocked?"

"Maybe, but he would have likely bought 'em for us anyway."

"We wouldn't a ratted on him in a million years."

"Not in a zillion."

"He's too good a guy."

"Sure is."

Cates moved to the other side of the table and chalked up his cue. Frank picked up his stick and resumed the game, making a long corner shot and then an easy one in the other corner. He was sighting in a bank shot in the side, when the back door opened again, this time letting in Tony Ruglia.

"Hey, Tone." Cates saluted with his cue.

"Hey, guys, how's it going?"

"How are you, Tony?" Frank stood up by the table.

"You'll never guess who I saw at All-American Market." Tony walked over to Cates.

"Who?"

"Billy Cotton."

"When?"

"Half hour, maybe forty-five minutes."

Cates and Frank pointed their cues at each other.

"Let's go."

They tossed their cues on the table and ran for the back door. The kids at the other table looked around to see what all the fuss was about.

"Wait for me, guys." Tony hurried for the back door. "I'll go with you."

42

SORRY, GUYS." TEDDY MARTINEZ LEANED against the cash register in his store. "He was here, but he's been gone at least forty-five minutes. You were here then, Tony."

"I told 'em. It's over forty-five minutes now."

"We had to start somewhere." Cates explained.

"What's the big deal anyway? Why do you want to see Billy Cotton so bad?"

"Frankie here's lived in Cotton for two years and he's never even seen him."

"Is that right?"

"Yeah. I've never seen the guy."

"Let's check Dale's." Cates suggested.

"Okay. See you, Teddy."

"See you Frank, fellows. Don't forget the election coming up."

"We can't vote." Tony called back over his shoulder.

"Tell your folks to vote. For me."

When the boys entered Dale Honeycutt's barber shop just up and across the street from the All-American Market, Dale was half-asleep sitting in one of his own barber chairs. The place was empty.

"Hey, hey, what?" The clanging bell on the door roused him. "What the hell?"

"Hey, Dale." Frank puffed out a greeting.

"Damn, what's the matter with you kids? World War III break out or what?"

"We just ran over from the All-American. We're looking for Billy Cotton. You seen him?"

"Hell, no, he wouldn't come in a low class place like this. He acts like Cotton ain't good enough for him anymore. That's what's wrong with America today. It's Kennedy and the damn Democrats. Everybody thinks they're. . . ."

"Too good to work." Frank finished the sentence. "Right?"

"That's right. Lazy bastards."

"Uh, see you, Dale." Frank backed Tony out the door and pulled Cates with him. "We gotta go."

"So long, Dale."

"Yeah, yeah."

"We'll tell Billy hello for you if we find him."

"You can tell him to go to hell as far as I'm concerned." Dale watched the boys charge out the door.

"Where to now?"

"I don't know. It doesn't look promising." Tony looked up and down the street.

"I know." Cates suggested. "The hardware store."

"It's gonna close any minute." Tony warned.

"Well, let's make like the wind and blow." Frank snickered.

"Let's make like a sheepherder and get the flock out of here." Cates countered.

"Let's make like a tree and leaf." Tony joined in.

With a burst of energy the trio ran down the sidewalk toward the hardware store laughing happily.

"He ain't been in here, man." Art Vasquez was behind the counter at Valley Hardware. "Why would he come here?"

"We don't know, Ese." Frank looked around the store as if Billy Cotton might be hiding somewhere in the back. "We're just trying to find him."

"You guys need some twenty-two shells?" Art peeked over at Harry Jacobs, the store manager. Harry gave him a boss-like frown.

"Yeah, that'd be good." Cates held his arms up like he was holding a rifle. "If we find Billy C. we'll just shoot him. That way Mason can finally meet him."

"Where to now?"

"Heck. I don't know."

"How about if we drive around and look for him?"

"You got gas money?"

"I can give you fifty cents."

"Tony?"

"No deal, guys. I've known Billy Cotton for years. I'm not going to run around town looking for him and wasting gas."

"Make it sixty cents."

"Let's do it." Cates grabbed the change.

After Tony left, they got Cates's Merc and pumped a buck's worth of gas into it and started cruising Cotton. They went by the fire station, by the park, up to the school, and back around the neighborhoods. They saw no sign of Billy C. It was nearly dark when they drove out to the highway, then back down Annie Bishop's street. She stood out in her front yard. Cates pulled over.

"What are you doing?" Frank slid down in the seat.

"Let's say hi to Annie, maybe she's seen Billy."

"Damn, what if her jerk boyfriend is here?"

"Who cares."

"Hi, guys." Annie walked out to the curb. She came right up to Frank's window. He gave her a weak smile.

"Where's Cassius Clay?" Cates teased her.

"Who?"

"Your new beau, the boxer."

"Oh, I'm so sorry about that, Jimmy. I don't know what came over David. He's not usually like that, really."

"It's all right. Nobody much got hurt. I think Frankie here got the worst of it and he wasn't even in the fight."

Annie put her hand on Frank's arm. He flinched slightly. She lifted her hand. He looked into her eyes and tried to make his own express an apology. He wanted to speak it out loud, felt it well inside. But with Cates beside him it was impossible. She broke eye contact and stepped back

"We gotta go. It's getting late. We just wanted to say hi."

"Okay, guys, bye-bye."

Annie looked down at Frank and winked. Cates eased the Merc out and pulled away. They turned at the first corner and headed toward the fire station.

"Well, shit a brick." Cates slapped the steering wheel. "We forgot to ask her about Billy C."

"That was the only reason we stopped."

"What a couple of spazzes, wanna go back?"

"No, no, let's go on."

"Okay."

"Let's just make another round and then call it quits."

"Good enough."

"Look over there." They had reached Main and passed the fire station. "Isn't that King Cotton himself in front of the Legion hall?"

"By doggies, it is." Cates slowed. "Should we ask him?"

"I don't know. He's kind of mean, ain't he?"

"You scared of that old man?"

"No, but I don't know him."

"Me neither." Cates stopped the Merc by the curb. King Cotton stood under the light in front of the hall smoking a cigar. "Go ask him."

"You."

"Go on, he ain't gonna bite you."

"Damn."

Frank eased out of the car. He paused a moment, then forced himself to walk over to King Cotton.

"Uh, Mr. Cotton."

"Huh?"

"Mr. Cotton, my name's Frank Mason." King looked him up and down.

"Kate Mason's boy?"

"Yes, sir."

"What can I do for you, son?"

"Sir, uh, we, my friend and I were looking for your son and wondered if you might know where he is?"

"You friends with Billy?"

"Well… maybe sort of."

"Maybe sort of, huh? Well, I'm sorry to disappoint you, but Billy's already come and gone."

"Gone?"

"He just came down for the day. He's gone back up to San Diego. Left a little while ago."

"Oh." Frank excused himself and slowly walked back to the car.

"Well?"

"He seems like a nice man."

"I mean Billy C."

"He already left."

"Already left? When?"

"I don't know. Some time ago."

"You don't seem interested anymore."

"No reason to be, now. Seems kind of silly to have been running around all over town for a guy we hardly know and is so hard to find he might as well not even exist."

"Weird. A minute ago it was like the most important thing in the world." Frank raised both hands palms up.

Cates revved up the Merc, burnt a U in the middle of Main Street and headed back toward the four-way intersection. They passed the police station on the Legion side of the fire station. There were no cops in sight.

"You better watch it, or you'll get a ticket driving like this in front of the John Laws."

"You are really strange sometimes, Mason. Did you know that?"

"Maybe."

Frank stared out the window. Cates glanced over.

"I tell you what, I'm going up to Jackson's and get me some fries or something. You can come if you want to, or you can stew about not seeing Billy or whatever it is that you stew about. You coming or not?"

"I'm going."

There wasn't a cop down on the corner either and no traffic, so Cates rolled through the four-way and then put the gas to the Merc for the short block to Jackson's. He parked in the empty dirt lot east of the café and shut off the engine.

"Well?"

"Well, what?"

"We gonna go in and get some chow, or ain't we?"

"I'm broke now, I gave you my money for gas."

"For crying out loud. I'll spring for fries. Jeez."

"All right, take it easy."

"You take it easy."

"Okay, mister." Frank, seemingly and suddenly back in good spirits, challenged. "Last one in, Jinx, you owe me a Coke." He opened the door and jumped out of the car.

"There you go." Cates followed suit. "That's more like it. That's the Mason I know."

They slammed the car doors shut and raced into Jackson's. Light from the café briefly filtered out into the dark. The streets of Cotton were empty and quiet. Night was settling on the valley.

43

SHREVE WAS EXHAUSTED. IT HAD been a long day and all he wanted was to finish up, grab some beer, and go home to his trailer where he could put his feet up and relax. Driving down a dirt road beside one of his fields, the hot wind blasting him in the face, he saw something under a trailer at the head of the field. He slowed down to see better. It looked like somebody.

He stopped the pickup and got out, leaving the truck running and the door open. He climbed down into and out of the drainage ditch between the road and the field and walked quietly up behind the trailer.

"Having a good time down there?"

Lane woke with a start and not realizing where he was, tried to jump up. He banged his head on the bottom of the trailer and stepped on his straw work hat.

"Damn." He came out into the sunlight cursing and rubbing his head. "Son of a bitch, West, you could have given me some warning."

"I didn't want to screw up your beauty rest."

"So, what's up? Time to quit?" He picked up his straw hat, dusted it off, and tried it on gingerly.

"Looks like it already is for you."

"Heck, boss. I was just taking a little break, that's all."

"You take a lot of little breaks. You want to keep this job, you're gonna have to spend less time on breaks and more time working. You understand?"

"Hell, boss, I do my work. 'Sides, there's plenty of wetbacks to do the shit work. Most of this crap ain't fit for no white man to do."

"Stop calling me boss, and these fields don't know what color a man is that's working 'em. Work is work, for Mexican or for white. You're getting paid to do a job, so do it and stop your loafing and complaining. You don't hear Cesar and Leon griping, do you?"

"They can't complain, they don't talk nothing but Mexican."

"You just do your job and don't worry about other folks."

"Oh, sure, that's easy for you to say. You got it made. You get everything handed to you on a silver platter."

"What does that mean?"

"You know what it means."

"No, I don't. Suppose you explain it to me."

"You don't have to play the goody goody around me." Lane looked over Shreve's shoulder. "I know what's up."

"You know what's up? What is up?"

"It don't take a genius to see why you're the crew chief and the rest of us are just peon workers. Everybody knows you're banging Marcie Cotton Clayborn."

"Maybe you know too much about my life, Mr. Genius. And you leave Marcie Clayborn out of it."

"Hey, hey. I got nothing against it. She's a good-looking piece. Wouldn't mind banging her myself—"

Shreve cut him off with an open-palmed slap across the side of the face.

"Hey, what the hell." Lane covered up.

Shreve cuffed him several more times, slapping and pushing him back against the trailer. "You keep your nose out of my business and don't ever say anything about Marcie to me again."

"Just because you're crew chief don't give you the right to push me around. Maybe Jeff would want to know about you and his wife."

Lane tried to duck, but a lightning right cross caught him flush in the left temple and sent him sprawling in the dirt beside the trailer. Shreve immediately grabbed him and jerked him to his feet.

"You pissant." He held him by the shirt collar. "I ought to beat your scummy butt to a pulp."

He drew back his right hand. Lane flinched and held up an arm in defense. Shreve pushed him up against the trailer.

"I don't ever want to see you around here again. And if you say anything to Jeff Clayborn I'll stick this trailer up your ass. Understood?"

"Okay, okay." Lane held his arms up in surrender.

Shreve let go his hold. Lane immediately punched him, the blow knocking Shreve backward. He recovered quickly and fired a hard right into Lane's stomach, doubling him up. He followed with a left hook to the jaw and then a straight right that bloodied Lane's nose and knocked him to his knees where he knelt, stunned. Shreve stepped up and pushed him over with his boots, then bent down and spoke in a hard, emotionless voice.

"Never—*ever*—fuck with me again. You understand?"

Turning on his heels, he headed back toward the truck. He scrambled over the ditch, hopped in the pickup and drove away, dust boiling up behind in a swirling, brown cloud.

Back by the trailer, Lane rolled over in the dirt holding his jaw. He pulled himself up to his knees, coughed twice loudly, and spit blood onto the soft, sandy ground.

"Son of a bitch." He gestured in the general direction of Shreve's truck. "Crummy bastard."

44

FRANK WAS RAKING UP BRANCHES on the lawn when little old Mrs. Davis came hobbling out the door. He banged his rake on the ladder Uncle Carl stood atop trimming branches from a big palm tree in the middle of the front yard.

"Here's Mrs. Davis."

Carl let go of a branch, which landed several feet from Mrs. Davis.

"Watch it up there." The old lady swung her walking stick wildly about.

"What's that, Mrs. Davis?" Carl asked from the relative safety of the ladder.

Mrs. Davis limped out and Frank backed up a couple of steps. She squinted up at Carl.

"I said be careful."

Frank coughed to hide a laugh. Mrs. Davis gave him a severe look. The old lady turned back to the tree and ladder.

"You're trimming those branches too high up and you're cutting them too short."

"Yes, ma'am." Carl sawed another limb off exactly like he had all the others. But this time he held the cut branch, waiting for Mrs. Davis to get out of the way. She didn't budge.

"What did you say, Waters?"

"I said, yes, ma'am. Now please move so I can toss this branch down."

"Well."

She struggled out of harm's way. Carl tossed the branch down. Frank picked it up gingerly. He was always careful with palm tree branches. All it took was stabbing yourself once or twice with the sharp needles and you realized that cut palm branches were hardly passive refuse. They were downright dangerous and definitely painful.

"Excuse me, ma'am." He moved past Mrs. Davis to toss the branch onto the pile of palm cuttings, leaves, and dead grass he'd neatly raked and stacked next to the fence.

"Don't make a mess there, sonny."

"No, ma'am. We're gonna load it right on the trailer there and haul it off for you."

Carl began descending the ladder.

"Don't leave little piles of dirt and grass like you usually do."

"No, ma'am."

Frank hurried over to the ladder and braced it.

"We'll leave your place spick and span." Carl climbed off the ladder.

They carefully lowered the ladder, hauled it over and set it outside the fence by the trailer hooked up behind Carl's Jeep. Mrs. Davis kept an eagle eye on them until they loaded up the branches and grass and left her yard neat as a pin. They headed for the city dump east of Cotton.

"Does Mrs. Davis really think she owns the place, Uncle Carl?"

"I believe she does."

"She doesn't seem to know that you're the actual owner."

"I reckon not."

"You don't care?"

"Naw, it don't hurt nothing if she thinks it's her place. Shoot, she's lived there for years. And she's been in the valley as long as anyone else. They ain't no harm in it."

"That's neat of you."

Frank looked out the window at the fields rolling by and thought about Mrs. Davis and what she might have been like when both she and the valley were young. He couldn't seem to get a clear picture of it in his mind.

"Uncle Carl, what was the valley and Cotton like when you and Aunt Jean came out here?" Carl looked out his window, then back at the road.

"Mostly like it is now. Maybe the towns are some bigger, but it's mostly always been a farming place."

"The same for twenty years. That's impressive."

"Twenty-four. We came out before the war."

"Wow. That's a long time."

"Yep."

"You still like living here?"

"I never thought of it that way. It's just where we live, me and the old woman."

"How did you get your rental houses, like Mrs. Davis's?"

"That was from the money we got when our boy died."

"Oh, you mean Johnny D. You know I saw him once back home."

"Is that right?"

"He came to visit us out at Uncle Zack and Aunt Mary's. He brought a big old hunk of bologna that wasn't cut. I was real little, but I can still smell that bologna."

Carl was silent, his face revealing nothing extraordinary from the talk about his youngest boy's death on the cold hills of Korea. Even so, Frank changed the topic.

"So what do you think, can the Yanks come back and take the Dodgers?"

"I don't know. They're two games down already. And this Koufax feller's hot right now."

"Yeah, but the Yanks still have Mantle, and he's great."

"Can't argue that."

"The Yanks are the best."

A few minutes later, Carl turned the Jeep and trailer off the highway onto the dirt road leading to the dump. He was quieter, then, maybe thinking about his lost son and what he might have become if he'd had the chance to live out his life.

To fill up the dead air, Frank chattered about the World Series. He cited batting and earned run averages, home run and RBI totals, who played well and who didn't. He was good at baseball talk. He'd been speaking it for most of his life. He could do it for hours. Carl didn't stop him. He seemed content to let his nephew ramble on. After all, it didn't hurt anything.

45

"WANDA." KING COTTON CALLED FROM a window booth in Galvan's. "Get me some more coffee and bring the boy another plate of pancakes."

"Hold them pancakes, Wanda." Shreve sat across from the powerful landowner. "Lord, I'm so full now I'm about to bust."

"Go ahead, have a good breakfast. I want my new foreman strong and ready to work."

"Thank you, Mr. Cotton. I appreciate everything, but if I eat one more thing I'll pop right out of my shirt." Wanda was still waiting.

"Just the coffee." She poured a big cup, brought it over and set it in front of the old man then went back behind the counter. "We best enjoy ourselves while we can. I expect it's not going to be any easier with the next crop. This was the poorest cotton harvest in years. Without the fields you took care of, I don't believe I'd a made a dime. Barely did as it is. It was a close call this year."

"Just doing my job, Mr. Cotton."

"And a darn fine job, too."

"Thank you, sir."

"You know, though, son, I heard tell you had trouble with one of the boys on your crew. Is that right?"

"Well, sir. I took care of that."

"Maybe something else could have been done?"

"Lane was a lazy, complaining, good for nothing. He pushed me too far. Hell, my Mexicans worked circles around the guy."

"White men don't like to do this work no more."

"Then they shouldn't come looking for a handout. You take a job, do it or get out. It's simple."

"It's not always so simple for everybody."

"Maybe not."

"Jeff is mad about this Lane thing, and about your fields."

"What can I do about that?"

"I understand you not giving a damn about what Jeff thinks, but he's my son-in-law, married to my daughter, and I don't want him to think he's being replaced."

"I don't mean to take anybody's place."

"The way I want to work this, to make it the best all around, is for you to take care of my property up here by Northland."

"That's fine with me."

"Let me finish."

"Yes, sir."

"This way you should be able to stay out of Jeff's way. And vice versa. He can run his crews and you run yours, and nobody has to come head to head. Can you live with that?"

"Yes, sir."

"Good. And that way, too, you wouldn't have to take care of anything else that might belong to Jeff, you understand?"

Shreve looked up. King's cool, clear gaze let him know right away that the old man wasn't talking about farming. He was sharp as a tack still. Not much got past him.

"No, sir, Mr. Cotton. I guess I wouldn't have to. As long as he was taking care of it himself."

"Fair enough." King leaned back in the booth and rubbed his chin. Shreve rested his arms on the table. "Fair enough."

46

H OW COULD HE HAVE DONE this to me?" Jeff Clayborn
complained to Marcie as they drove to El Centro for supper. "That
guy ain't nothing but a stupid kid."

She looked out at the mostly harvested fields and sighed.

"It's not personal, Jeff. You must have learned that from Daddy by now.
Business is business, and farming is a business. You get the right people for the
right job. That's all."

"Of course you're gonna back your daddy."

"Don't pout and turn the air on." They neared the stockyard south of Cotton. "I don't want to smell all those damn stinky cows."

Jeff switched on the air conditioner as they approached the yard. "I'm tired
of putting up with all this bullshit."

"Oh, for heaven's sakes. What is your problem?"

"What's my problem? *My* problem?"

"Yes, *your* problem."

"*My* problem is your father making this boy the same as me, and the punk
ain't worked for us but four months."

"Same as you? So, Shreve's Daddy's partner now, too, is he?"

"You know what I mean."

"No, I don't. You're not threatened in any way. Daddy's not taking anything from you."

"Like that coon preacher that ran off with your stupid Ladies Club's money, huh?" Marcie flushed red but said nothing. "I still don't see why in the hell he did something like this. He must be getting feeble in his mind."

"That's the stupidest damned thing I've ever heard in my life. My daddy took my grandpa's farm over when it wasn't worth a dime and built it into what we have today. We, Jeff, you and me, all of us. You're damn lucky to be included in it. Papa's been generous with you. He made you his partner, taught you the business, and now you repay him with your petty whining."

"He made his money off Uncle Sam." Jeff sneered as they passed the Brawley city limits sign. "Everybody knows that."

"And you'd still be making yours picking tomatoes. Like you were when Daddy found you."

"So what?"

"Damn it, Jeff, Shreve is in the same place you were once. A kid trying to make it and willing to do what has to be done to get there. You should be able to understand that."

"Shreve, Schmeve, you sure like to say his name a lot."

"It is his name."

"You know if I didn't know better I'd say you were sweet on that boy."

"And if I didn't know better, I'd say you had a little whore giving you what you haven't wanted from me for years."

Jeff's ears reddened. For a moment, he looked like he might be considering a comeback but settled for a disgusted, what-do-you-know grunt instead. Marcie went back to watching out the window at the broad fields rolling by. They drove through Brawley and Imperial and on into El Centro without saying another word.

47

LAR TURNER HAD ALREADY MADE a couple of mid-morning runs through the black and migrant worker neighborhoods east of the tracks but there was nothing going on except for kids playing and women doing wash, so he leisurely cruised back downtown thinking of Carol Scott. Lately Carol had begun to avoid him, to refuse him her favors. Even when he threatened her, she still said no.

"Have to get me another one." He did a California rolling stop at the intersection of Main and the highway. "What I need is a grown-up woman. Like Marcie Clayborn or Manny Ruiz's hot little bitch. Ooh, I bet she'd go off like a Mexican jumping bean."

He was thinking of Manny Ruiz's wife sitting astraddle of him as he passed the American Legion hall and the Baptist Church which he attended briefly when he first moved to Cotton. He drove on toward CHS, the airport on his right, and slowed down in front of the new multi-purpose building. There were several junior and senior girls out front, but even when he stopped in the street, they wouldn't come out and talk to him. Things were changing in Cotton and he didn't like it much.

"Stuck up little bitches." It was almost loud enough for the girls to hear. "You don't know what you're missing."

Peeling rubber, he roared past the school out into the country toward King Cotton's place. He slowed up passing King's and imagined himself a successful farmer. Sometimes he thought about trying to get a small place, maybe settle down and raise a kid or two. But that was only wishing. He'd never be able to get any kind of place on his measly policeman's salary.

Cursing Bob Lowell's cheapskate style of city management, he took a back road that ran between a series of lettuce and onion fields. The road dead-ended three miles north of Cotton at a blacktop road leading west to the Salton Sea, east to the highway. Lar turned right toward the highway.

Rapping the squad car out, he roared down the blacktop, wheels whining on the smooth asphalt surface. Skidding up to the stop sign at the highway, he was about to pull out when a beat up old Ford sedan rattled past doing ninety to nothing and weaving from side to side.

He tore after the Ford, lights flashing and siren blaring. He chased it toward Cotton, amazed that it could go as fast as it did, blue smoke boiling out behind from an engine that had to be missing like a sailor gone AWOL.

He put his foot to it and got right on the Ford's tail. He stayed there as it slowed down nearing Cotton and finally pulled over onto the shoulder of the road. Sliding to a stop, he parked about thirty feet behind, got out, ticket book in hand, and swaggered up to the driver's side of the Ford.

He walked right up to the window and leaned down. The driver was a scrawny, scraggly-toothed man of indeterminate age. Even though the car had California plates, Lar figured the guy for an out-of-work ridgerunner or Okie. Probably moved out west looking for the same pie in the sky easy money his Dust Bowl relatives had twenty-five years before.

"You got a license?" He frowned at the skinny, sun-browned man.

"Yeah, yeah, sure."

While the man dug in the glove compartment, Lar prided himself on so swiftly and deftly recognizing the man for who and what he was.

"Here you go." The man held out the papers, smiling.

Lar reached in for the license but what he saw was a flash of blue steel and fire. A popping sound echoed through the quiet streets on the north side of Cotton. Something heavy hit him in the chest. As he fell backward, a confused look on his face, he saw the skinny man's face staring back at him, grinning distortedly.

Abruptly, the Ford, engine sputtering, spun around on the shoulder and shot back onto the highway heading back in the direction it had come, toward Northland. In a moment it was out of sight. Behind, dust swirled up alongside the road, hanging in the still valley morning air like an indifferent brown shroud over Lar Turner's lifeless body.

48

FRANK STOOD AT THE BOTTOM of the steps in front of the Baptist church trying to decide whether to go in or not. He could just barely hear the preacher delivering the service, not well enough to make out the words, only the solemn tone. While he stood there, trapped between aversion and guilt, the front door of the church opened and, to his complete surprise, Marcie Clayborn stepped out.

She saw him right away.

"Hi."

"Hi." He looked away from her steady gaze. "Is the service over?"

"No, but I'd heard enough. One more 'The Lord works in mysterious ways' or 'It's all part of His divine plan' and I would have probably done or said something I'd regret later."

"Did you know Lar well?"

"Well enough."

"Oh."

"Was he your friend?"

"Sort of."

"Well, it's too bad when anybody dies."

"Yeah, I guess so."

"Still, when it comes to the balancing of accounts, maybe Lar's dying evens something up."

Frank wondered if she knew the stuff about Lar and Carol or the things that Sandra had told him. The latter certainly seemed unlikely. Yet Marcie seemed to know everything about everybody in Cotton. At least that was what people said.

"Well, I've paid whatever respects I needed to pay." Frank looked down at the pavement. "It's not a crime if you don't, you know. It's okay to have mixed feelings about things." It took a minute for her meaning to sink in.

"Oh, I. . . ."

"Listen, maybe I'll have some work for you and your uncle out at my place one of these days. You still work with him on the weekends?"

"Yes, ma'am."

"Marcie, call me Marcie. Don't you dare call me ma'am again. Aren't you aware that a young woman hates to be treated like an old dowager?" She smiled to let him know she was teasing. "Maybe I'll see you soon."

She turned and walked toward her car, parked just around the corner.

"Bye-bye."

"Bye."

Frank watched her walk away. She was adult-looking and mature in her mourning clothes, yet so pretty and shapely with a sleek, swishing gait. He couldn't take his eyes off her as she gracefully climbed into her big Olds. She turned the car around and drove back down Main in front of the church. She rolled the window down, flashed one of her heartbreaking smiles and winked. He blushed and looked away, but after she passed, he walked to the curb and watched the Olds until it reached the four-way stop at the highway, paused briefly, then turned left toward Northland, disappearing behind the dusty, decaying buildings of downtown Cotton.

49

WELL, WELL." DALE HONEYCUTT POINTED as Cates came into the barber shop. "If it isn't Mr. Big Shot, Mr. El Centro."

"What do you say, Dale?"

"What can I do you for today?"

"Just a haircut."

"I'm here to serve." Dale indicated the closest barber chair with a sweep of his arms.

Cates sat down.

"How's the job?"

"Can't complain. One-sixty an hour, time and a half for overtime when I start full time."

"Not bad, not bad."

"So, Dale, I haven't been in town much lately, what's the word on Lar getting shot? They haul anybody in yet?"

"Hell, no, this bunch of incompetents? They'll probably never find the guy."

"They hire anybody to take over for him?"

"Nah, nobody thought of that yet, I don't imagine. Who would want the job, anyway?"

"Sure was weird though, huh? It happening right before Hallowe'en and all."

"Yeah." Dale combed Cates' hair and then clipped some off the top. "But as far as I'm concerned, it's just proof of what I been saying all along, the country's getting more screwed up every day."

"You really think so? I bet people have always said that about whatever time they lived in."

"Maybe, but looks to me like we're going straight to hell."

"Could be."

"Did you hear what that Glover girl did the other night at the Legion?"

"Sandra? No, what?"

"She was giving some kind of talk up there. I don't know why."

"What'd she say?"

"They say she blamed all the colored's problems on white people. Can you imagine that? Kennedy's to blame for that kind of bull in my opinion."

"I don't know, Sandra's always had a mind of her own."

"At least it got the city bigwigs all in a huff. Then old Teddy Martinez comes in here saying if he gets elected he's going to try to get her to work for the council. Crap."

He finished the hair cutting and got out a pair of electric clippers to trim around the ears and the back of the neck.

"Teddy might have thought she'd help him get votes with the coloreds and Mexicans. He's really hot about being mayor."

"Malarkey. Teddy just wants to get her sweet ass poon." Dale set the clippers down, slapped some stinky hair oil on his hands and ran it through Cates' hair before combing it again. Then he swung him around to face the row of mirrors lining the room in back of the barber chairs.

"What do you think?"

"That's just fine, thanks."

He unpinned the covering sheet, lifted it carefully and popped it, the cut hair falling to join the little piles of hair already on the otherwise clean floor.

"That'll be three bits."

Cates handed him a dollar. "Keep the change."

"Big spender."

"Say. Did you hear they're thinking about reopening the movie house?"

"The one here in Cotton?"

"Yeah, the old one around the corner."

"It's the only one around the corner and there's about as much chance of that happening as Lar Turner coming back from the dead."

Dale seemed to think that was a good joke.

"I guess so."

"We'll see you later, then."

"See you later, and thanks."

Outside, Cates turned right and headed west toward the four-way stop. When he reached the corner, he looked north and saw the place about where Lar had been killed. He imagined the policeman lying by the road, blood pumping from his exploded heart. With no small effort, he drove that terrible image from his mind and walked on.

50

SHREVE ROLLED OVER ON HIS back and looked at the ceiling above Marcie's bed, clenching his jaw muscles.

"What's the matter, baby?" She turned to see his face in profile, laid her right hand on his chest. "It happens sometimes, that's all. You had a hard day at work and rushed to get here. It could happen to anybody."

"I don't know, Marcie, I don't think I. . . ."

"Shh, don't say anything. It's okay."

"You don't know what I was going to say."

"I don't want to."

"What do you mean?"

"Maybe this is as far as it—*we*—can go."

"You mean *done?*"

"Are we?"

"I don't know, Marcie." Shreve rubbed his chin with his thumb and forefinger. She sat up in bed, held a pillow against her bare chest.

"One of these days you'll find you a good girl, and she'll make you the kind of wife you want and need."

"You're amazing." He rolled over, laid his arm across her leg. She played with the hair on his arm.

"Maybe a girl like Carol Scott."

"Carol Scott?"

"Why not?"

"She's Billy's girl."

"Oh, honey, that was a long time ago. He didn't even look her up when he made his hit and run visit back at the end of summer."

"I thought her and Billy would get married when he got out of the service. She's always been Billy's girl."

"She doesn't know whose girl she is."

Marcie got out of bed and slipped on a light, sleeveless nightgown. Shreve watched her walk back and forth in the room picking up their clothes.

"Maybe I'll be better next week." He sat up in bed.

"I'm sorry, honey." She paused to look him straight in the eye. "I'm going to be out of town next week. We're going up to San Diego."

"Oh."

He got up, found his jeans and slipped into them. She had disappeared into the bathroom across from the bed. He sat in a chair for a moment and looked around the empty room. After a couple of moments, he put on his shoes and socks and headed out the back door.

51

O N ELECTION DAY FRANK DITCHED school. He loafed
around the apartment all morning, catching up on neglected home-
work and listening to music on the radio. In the afternoon he went
out, roaming Cotton's streets and stopping in its businesses, visiting people he
hadn't seen for a while, and making occasional trips to the American Legion
Hall where his mother and Aunt Jean helped monitor the voting. Walking back
uptown from the Legion Hall an hour or so before the polls closed, he ran into
his Uncle Carl coming out of the post office.

"Hey, you."

"Hey, boy." Carl flashed a wide grin, the unmistakable odor of alcohol es-
caping with it.

"What'ya doing up here?"

"I was looking for the old woman, but the windows are closed and don't
seem to be nobody there. Wasn't no mail in the box."

"It's election day. They've been closed all day. I didn't even know the outside
door would be open. Somebody must've forgot to lock it."

"Oh, I see."

"Aunt Jean's at the American Legion working on the voting stuff. She and
Mom have been there all day."

"I plumb forgot."

"You gonna vote?"

"I reckon not." Carl took off his baseball cap and ran a thick-fingered hand through his thinning hair.

"You're not, really?"

"Hell, can't say's I've voted since I wasn't much older'n you."

"You must've voted for Roosevelt?"

"Once, but, hell, I ain't voted since. There ain't no need. My vote ain't gonna matter one way or the other. The whole thing's out of my hands."

"What if everybody felt that way?"

"I guess nobody'd vote."

Frank scratched his head. He wasn't sure what to make of such heretical ideas. He wasn't sure Uncle Carl was serious. He was sure the older man was a little tipsy. He wrote the heresy off to drink.

"You gonna go by the Legion?" Carl made some tentative motions to leave.

"Reckon so."

"We'll see you, Uncle Carl."

"So long, boy."

He walked across the street to his Jeep. Frank strolled on up to the four-way and crossed over to the other side of the highway. As he passed York's Electric and neared Chuy's Bar, the door opened and Chuy himself came out, accompanied by a man Frank didn't know. They were engaged in an energetic conversation. He caught some of it as they walked by.

"You don't know what you're talking about." The big man wagged a finger at Chuy.

"Ten to one on Martinez."

"Bull."

"Put your money where your mouth is."

"Hell, I didn't think you gave a rat's ass about this stuff. I thought politics was nothing but a big game."

The men were getting out of earshot now, but Frank wanted to hear what Chuy said so he stopped and looked back as they walked away.

"Hell." Chuy declaimed. "You know damn well if voting meant anything, they'd make it against the law."

He and the big man went on their way. Frank continued on toward Jackson's Café. From there he crossed the street and went into the All-American Market. A highly agitated Teddy Martinez paced back and forth by the registers.

"Hey, Teddy, how's it going?"

Teddy chewed his nails. "What's the word from the polls? What's going on? Have you been there?"

"Not even closed yet. Nothing's been counted."

"Did you vote for me?" He whirled to face Frank.

"I can't vote for you. I'm too young."

"How about your mom? Your aunt and uncle?"

"I didn't ask, but they probably voted for you."

"Great." Teddy popped his right fist into his open left palm. "That's good news." He looked genuinely relieved.

"I heard if you win, you're gonna get Sandra Glover a job working for the council. Is that right?"

"You bet. Sharp young girl. She'll be mayor here someday."

"Wow."

"So, you going back to the hall soon?"

"In a little bit. I think I'll get something to eat and drink first."

"Wish me luck?"

"Good luck."

He gave Teddy the high sign and walked back outside. With nearly an hour yet to kill, he decided to go to Jackson's and get some food.

It was cool and quiet in the cafe and he found a booth in back by the kitchen where he'd worked as a dishwasher for a few months his first year in Cotton. He ordered a burger, fries, and Coke and while he waited, plugged a quarter in the juke box up front and selected the Rooftop Singers' hot new hit and a couple of up-tempo Beach Boys records.

After he ate, he stayed on a while more, playing another quarter's worth of tunes and chatting with the new dishwasher, an older guy who'd just moved to town from Yuma. When the supper business started picking up, he paid his bill and left. The polls would be closed by the time he got to the Legion hall, so he headed straight there.

At the hall, the vote count was under way. Everyone was busy, so he stayed out of the way, content to stand to one side beneath a painting of President Kennedy and watch the proceedings. At one end of the voting room was a big blackboard on which Manny Ruiz tallied the votes for Mayor Lowell or Teddy Martinez as each ballot box was emptied, sorted, counted, and then recounted. Manny took his job seriously and from time to time would utter declamations on the election process.

"The American system at work." He chalked up a large number of votes for Teddy. "This is what I call democracy. . . freedom in action. . . great turn out, best in years. . . everybody should vote, if they don't, they shouldn't complain about the way things are going, right?" He looked right at Frank, who made the high sign before heading over to the table where his mother had been tabulating votes.

"Looks like Teddy's going to get his wish, huh, Mom?"

"Sure does."

"He's a good guy."

"Yes, he is, but so is Bob Lowell."

"We couldn't lose, could we?"

"Nope."

"Mrs. Mason." Manny called over. "Can you give us a hand on this recount?"

"Be right there."

"I'll see you back home, Mom."

"Okay, son."

Frank hung out a few minutes more until he was certain Teddy would win, then headed back home. He walked through the park alongside the police station in the dark. He crossed Church Street and passed underneath one of Cotton's rare streetlights. His shadow danced ghostly upon the dirt and weeds of the empty, scrub field running alongside the sidewalk. He was too absorbed in his own thoughts to notice.

52

AROUND TEN-THIRTY, MARCIE CAME out in the front yard where Frank and Uncle Carl were busy trimming trees and asked Carl if he could run to town on an errand for her.

"Of course, Mrs. Clayborn, be glad to."

"Frank can stay here while you're gone."

"I'll be back in a little while." Carl unhooked the trailer from the Jeep.

"Okay. I'll just keep working."

Carl had been gone about five minutes when Marcie, wearing shorts and a low cut blouse, opened the door and came back outside

"Would you like a little break and something to drink?"

He leaned his rake against a nearby tree. "That'd be nice."

"What would you like? Water, ice tea, beer?"

"Do you have a Coke?"

"A Coke it is. Come on in."

Wiping his boots on the welcome mat, he followed Marcie inside. It was cool in the house and he detected pleasant, though undifferentiated, odors.

While she made the Coke, putting lots of ice in the glass, he stood by the kitchen table, trying unsuccessfully not to look awkward and ill at ease. She brought the Coke to him with a big smile.

He couldn't keep his eyes off her cleavage and the glass nearly slipped out of his hand.

"Be careful, you almost dropped that."

"Sorry, Mrs., uh—" She gave him a stern look. "*Marcie.*"

He took a big drink of the Coke. She watched him, still smiling. He tried to combat a growing erection by thinking of how cold the ice in the glass was against his teeth. She walked over to the kitchen sink. He downed the rest of the Coke.

"Frank." She opened the cabinet doors below the sink. "Could you help me get this trash up from underneath here and haul it away with your load?"

He set his glass on the table.

"You bet."

She pulled a large plastic trashcan out of the cabinet, knocking some paper onto the kitchen floor. He hurried over to help. They bent down together and he could see down the front of her blouse. He could see both of her breasts completely. He stared at them in a near state of catatonia. All he could move were his hands, and they clumsily pushed the paper around without being able to pick it up.

His face and hers were inches apart and when he tore his eyes away from her breasts, she was looking directly into his. They stood up, leaving the loose trash where it was. She stood so close to him he could feel her breasts against him and smell her clean hair. He gave up trying to control or hide his erection.

She leaned forward and kissed him lightly on the lips. He didn't move, standing rigid as a guard at Buckingham Palace. She kissed him lightly again, then more forcefully. He found himself unable to resist her, yielding to her firm, gentle lips. He could barely breathe.

"M—Marcie." He pulled away from her last kiss. "You're, er—married." She stayed close to him, her body pressing against his.

"They said you were the smart one."

He leaned away. She gave him a hurt look.

"Don't you like me?"

"I think you're wonderful, Mrs. Clayborn, but you're married. It's wrong."

"Is it wrong for two people who like each other to express affection?"

Her proximity made it hard for him to think at all, much less concoct moral arguments in favor of monogamy. She kissed him again, but he froze up like before, fear and slavish adherence to old codes winning out over natural impulse. She stepped back and studied his face. He looked away.

"You really are young, aren't you, honey?"

"I'm eighteen."

"For a boy who's been to Mexicali, you're new to things, aren't you?"

"I don't know."

Sighing, he realized that whatever might have happened between them, now wouldn't. He had blown it. Knowing that both relieved and depressed him. She went to the refrigerator, got the Coke out again and filled his glass.

"You need to get out and live some, baby." She handed him the glass of soda. "You've got a chance to turn out to be a good man, but you're still too wrapped up in notions about what's supposed to be and what's not."

He bit his lower lip.

"And don't get hung up feeling sorry for yourself. Life is just what it is. When things come along, you need to grab them. If you don't like what you get, change it, or change yourself. But whatever you do, live. Don't let what everybody else tells you ruin your life. Your life is yours and nobody else's. And it's a good life. You've got good friends, a good family. That's more than a lot of people can say. Maybe it'll take you a bit longer than most to really understand that. But the first step is to take your show on the road. There are a lot of great things going on outside of this valley, and you've got to find them on your own."

"Yes, ma'am—I mean, Marcie." He was filled to overflowing with this beautiful woman's vision of his own life.

"Now get out of here. I've talked way too much and you're not getting any work done. Your Uncle Carl will think you've turned into a bum." She kissed him on the cheek.

He guzzled down his Coke refill and went back to work. He was completely in love with Marcie now, but in a good way. She was a true, grownup, fabulous woman. He would never forget her or this day.

After lunch, as he and Carl loaded the trailer for a run to the dump, she came out of the house now wearing a light yellow summer dress. She climbed into the big Olds and with a wave for them drove off to town.

"That's one fine lady there, ain't she?"

Frank watched the Olds rolling down the road toward the highway. He recalled the feel of her lips on his.

"She sure is, Uncle Carl. She sure as heck is."

53

CATES WENT FROM BUILDING TO building at VJC looking for Frank. He made two passes through the packed student union where dozens of students crowded around a radio hooked up at one of the tables just outside the cafeteria. He ran into Sandra Glover and Tony Ruglia but they hadn't seen Frank. Tony thought he might have ditched school to shoot snooker over at a pool hall in Imperial. He shot pool about as often as he attended classes.

"Picked a hell of a day for it."

"He might be here." Tony indicated the general vicinity of the union. "We just haven't seen him."

"I'm going to look for him some more. Keep track of what's going on, okay?"

"We will." Sandra's eyes were red from crying.

Cates made another round and found him coming out of Humanities class.

"Mason, Mason." Frank looked up, spotted his buddy running toward him.

"Hey, Jimmy. What's up?"

"Did you hear the news?"

"What news?" Frank grinned. He felt another Cates rumor coming on.

"The President's been shot." His smile disappeared.

"What are you talking about?"

"It's on the radio, somebody shot President Kennedy down in Texas."

"Jimmy, if this is another one of your damn rumors, it isn't funny."

"I swear to you, Frank, you can hear for yourself over at the union."

"You're shitting me."

"C'mon, buddy. Tony and Sandra are already over at the union. They're broadcasting live."

"Who shot him?" The boys hurried towards the union.

"They don't know but a bunch of shots were fired, I think."

At the union they found Tony and Sandra and an ever-growing throng of students forming up around the radio. There were a lot of low, excited conversations going on among the crowd until someone called for silence.

"Quiet everybody, listen. Listen."

They all shoved closer to the radio to hear the news report. The newsman's voice crackled over the airwaves.

"Doctors at Parkland Memorial Hospital in Dallas, Texas, have just announced that President John F. Kennedy died from gunshot wounds at twelve-thirty p.m. local time."

The buzzing among the students stopped. No one said a word. A few people began to cry. The news report continued live from Dallas. Nobody went to class.

54

ANNIE BISHOP COULDN'T CONCENTRATE ON the preacher for the terrible images that kept popping up in her mind. Just yesterday she, and millions of others, had watched the man they said killed the president shot to death himself on national television. It made her shudder to remember it.

The community church was packed for the memorial service for the slain president and the minister filled the air with platitudes and homilies. Annie used her seat in back to scan the crowd. She saw the new mayor and his wife in the front row sitting next to the old one and his wife. King Cotton was there, and Jeff and Marcie Clayborn. She saw many of her friends from school and on the other side of the church midway up, she spotted Frank Mason sitting by his mother and his aunt and uncle.

Seeing him from where she sat, looking so serious and attentive, made Annie remember when they had been together. He had been so kind at first, so affectionate. Just the opposite of David, who had been rough and insistent and then dropped her so quickly. He had moved back to New Mexico without even saying good-bye. She wondered if there was something about her that made boys so different from one another, like Frank and David, act so alike in the end.

She tried listening to the preacher, but thinking about the dead president was more than she could bear. She looked over at Frank again, studying his boyish profile for signs of what she really didn't know. At that moment he turned and caught her looking at him. She averted her eyes.

Why had he broken up with her?

Frank kept watching Annie even after she looked away. In the past year, he must have asked himself that question dozens of times. She was as sweet and loving a girl as any guy could ever expect to get. And yet he had left her. He wondered what it was that hardened his heart toward a girl like her.

Thinking of his heart reminded Frank of coming forward to be saved at the Church of the Nazarene back in his Ozarks hometown when he was about ten. The preacher there told the small group of faithful who came forward and knelt before the altar to open up their hearts and let Jesus come in. He had tried, with all the effort he could muster, even imagining a door opening in his heart, but he did not feel Jesus come in.

He pretended to be saved anyway, not wanting to appear foolish in front of the congregation, but he knew nothing had happened. Maybe there was some connection between that moment and how he treated Annie. If so, it was too subtle for him to grasp.

For a few moments he listened to the preacher, but all that did was remind him of why he'd quit church in the first place. Besides being self-contradictory and a refuge for hypocrites, he reasoned from the clarity of his untested, youthful vision, church and religion were unbelievably boring.

He looked around again, saw King Cotton and Jeff and Marcie. In the back he saw Dale Honeycutt, hunched over, a handkerchief in his hand. How strange. Dale was always the first to criticize JFK, but now he looked the saddest of all. That didn't make sense, or did it somehow?

Maybe, there was a lot of stuff he didn't know, didn't understand. He chided himself for not thinking about the dead president. It was his and his family's tragedy and that of the nation that mattered, not the personal complaints of a kid like himself.

He forced himself to give his full attention to the preacher.

"None of us can know what the Lord intends for us. He works in truly wondrous and mysterious ways. . . ."

Frank turned to see Marcie's reaction, saw a bitter smile on her beautiful face. He looked back at the preacher who still intoned about God's will. But the man might as well have been speaking into an empty cave as far as he was concerned. He didn't hear another word.

55

COTTON'S FLAGPOLE, RISING ONE HUNDRED and eighty-four feet from the desert floor to sea level, was decorated each year just after Thanksgiving with strands of colorful lights. It could be seen at night halfway to Brawley, looking like the world's largest Christmas tree. The lit up flagpole was one of Frank's favorite things from the moment he saw it during his first Christmas in the valley.

The lights had been on a couple of nights already when he decided to walk down and take a close-up look. They were a lot more impressive from a distance, three or four blocks away being the best location to get the full Christmas tree effect, but he liked to walk right up underneath them, too.

The flagpole was on the east side of the fire and police station, out in the park, maybe fifty yards from the Little League field where he and Richard used to play home run derby.

The coolness of the night, and the twinkling of the flagpole lights as they swayed in the light breeze, combined to produce in him a feeling of not unpleasant melancholia. There were times, he found, when having a little bit of the blues actually felt good. Tonight was one of those times.

He walked alone through the night, memories welling up inside. He reached the flagpole and looked up at the lights. The blue and red and green bulbs reminded him of Christmas trees when he was a little boy. Of one Christmas in particular.

He remembered standing at the back of a big fraternity house living room, staring at his shoes and feeling small and nervous. He peeked across the room at the other boys and girls drinking punch by the big Christmas tree. It was the biggest tree he had ever seen, full and green and smelling clean like the woods. He had never seen so many bulbs or lights on a tree before. There were a lot of presents under the tree, too, wrapped in colorful paper. He wondered if one of them would be for him.

And even though the clean, shiny-faced fraternity brothers were being nice to all the kids and the lure of an unexpected present held interest for him, he was still anxious for the party to be over. He heard the word "underprivileged" used a couple of times, and although he wasn't sure what it meant, he didn't think he wanted to be whatever it was, not if being it meant having to go to parties like this one without any of your friends or family.

Now, as he stared up at Cotton's flagpole lights, that memory from his youth drifted away. His Ozark home, half a country and two and a half years behind him, could have been light years away. The feelings of his first emotional summer in Cotton were dulled as well. He realized that the passage of time was not always bad, for though it stole the sharpness of good memories, it also blunted those of the bad.

He turned then and walked away from the flagpole, his mild case of the blues fading. He thought a snack and something to drink would top off the evening just fine. With a hop out into the street, he headed for Jackson's Cafe. Up by Manny Ruiz's market he paused and looked back at the flagpole. It looked great from there, really impressive. It made him feel proud to be from Cotton.

56

FRANK HAD JUST FINISHED A Coke when he saw a big, yellow CHS bus pull up across the street from Jackson's. The doors swung open and a group of students, including Art Vasquez, came rushing in.

"Hey, Mason. Art called over from the counter where he and the other kids collected a large number of sacked orders to go."

"What's up, *Ese?*"

"Preseason tourney in Holtville, it's gonna be great."

"Team look good?"

"CIF for sure. Maybe this year we'll win it all."

"Sounds great."

"Why don't you come on, man, it'll be fun."

"Like the old days."

"Yeah."

"I don't know. I graduated already."

"Don't sweat it, Frank. My cousin's driving. He won't care. C'mon."

He paid his bill quickly and, grabbing some of the bags, helped haul the food and drinks out to the bus. Inside, he saw several kids he knew from school and several more from the lower grades he hadn't known. Art took a seat up front by his cousin, the driver, so Frank went down the aisle looking for a seat.

As he passed some of the younger girls, they looked at him and giggled. He swelled his chest up and acted like he was cool. Then he spotted Karen Edwards. Sitting by herself. As he neared her, his nerves eliminating his "coolness," she looked up. He smiled, like an idiot he was sure. To his surprise, she scooted over and made room for him beside her.

"Hi."

"Hi." He plopped down awkwardly on the seat. "Thanks."

With a grinding of gears, the big bus coughed and roared and rolled on down the back highway to Holtville.

"I really like basketball, don't you?" The bus passed the outskirts of Cotton and rumbled on into the dark night.

"Uh-huh."

Up close, he saw that she was even prettier than she was from a distance, but there was a disturbing lack of spark in her dark blue eyes. Still, he had to concentrate in order not to be flabbergasted by her beauty in such proximity to him. He wished for all the world he could be cool with girls—like Shreve West.

"Our games are always really exciting." He knew that would not have been what Shreve would have said.

"Uh-huh."

He arched an eyebrow and was quiet for a while. She sat there calmly, a little smile on her full lips. He squirmed in his seat, searched for the right thing to say.

"So, what's old CHS like without the class of 'sixty-three? A lot quieter I bet, huh?"

He smiled stupidly, like a spasmo. She didn't seem to notice his discomfort or sense the idiocy he felt certain hung about him in a glowing aura. Instead, she started rattling on about CHS and her life there. He happily sat back in the seat and let her go.

"... and then Mrs. Nelson made us clean the whole Home Ec room, can you believe that... Donna and Tom got caught by Mr. Grant by the boy's restroom. .. Jerome would have come with me tonight, but his parents wouldn't let him. Isn't that awful, I feel. . . ."

"Jerome? Jerome who?"

"Jerome Beltran, of course, he and I are going steady now, didn't you know? Oh, I guess not, you're gone now. Well."

He leaned his head in his hand and stared blankly ahead. She rambled on.

Jerome Beltran? Jerome Beltran? The biggest sap at CHS. The guy was a complete lamebrain. A fleabag. He was stunned to find out that Karen Edwards, the prettiest girl at CHS, was going steady with this addlepate. His opinion of this gorgeous girl was undergoing a rapid transformation. If she liked Jerome Beltran, she must be about as deep as the water that wasn't running in a desert wash in August. Oh, man, how could he miss the boat by so much?

The girl hadn't completed five sentences before he knew that, pretty or not, his interest in her had gone as far as it could go—the appreciation of her physical appearance from a distance. This was the way it had always been, but now even the heat he felt had been taken out of it. He realized the truth beneath the worn out cliché—you can't judge a book by its cover.

Oddly, the effect liberated him from his usual social fetters. To his surprise, he joined her in facile, meaningless chatter all the rest of the way to the tournament. For one of the few times in his life, he felt like a skilled conversationalist. If anyone around them had been listening, they would have thought he and she had known each other for years and were the best of friends.

After the game, in which Cotton administered another of its merciless poundings to an inferior squad, he found a different seat on the bus. He sat by a quiet little freshman boy and didn't say a word all the way back to Cotton. Karen didn't seem to be aware that he wasn't sitting beside her now or remember that they had talked before. She and a sophomore girl whispered and giggled the entire return trip.

He remembered something Dale Honeycutt had once said. Be careful what you wish for, because you just might get it. As far as his interest in Karen went, that little aphorism couldn't have been more appropriate. He put his feet up against the seat in front of him and closed his eyes. All the way back to Cotton, he fantasized being with the more interesting females of his acquaintance, like Carol Scott, Annie Bishop, and, Marcie Cotton Clayborn.

57

THE OLIVE-DRAB VEHICLE STOPPED at the Cotton police station just long enough for its driver to get directions, then continued west on the highway out of town. King Cotton happened to be home eating lunch, not his usual habit, when the car pulled into his long gravel driveway.

"Mr. King, Mr. King." Eloisa, the housekeeper who'd looked out for the old man since his wife died, cried in her heavy accent. "A *carro* is coming."

"Who is it?" He cut a piece of fat off a big steak and pushed it to the edge of his plate.

"I don' know. Maybe one man. A soldier?"

"A soldier?" King perked up. "Is it Billy?"

"*No, señor.*" She watched a man, obviously not Billy, climb out of the vehicle. King frowned. The doorbell rang. Eloisa looked at King.

"Well, answer it, damn it. I ain't paying you to gawk at me."

"*Sí, señor.*" Eloisa headed off to the front living room of the massive house.

When his wife was still alive and the kids growing up, King built the house and kept putting additions on it until it was the biggest house in the north end. Now, with only he and the housekeeper, the house seemed oppressively grandiose.

Empty and useless.

As soon as Eloisa returned with the army man in tow, he sensed something was wrong. He dropped his fork onto his plate, the sound ringing in his ears.

"Mr. Cotton?"

King focused on all the chevrons on the sleeves of the soldier's uniform. "Yes."

"Please, sir. Perhaps you should stay seated."

"I can hear just as well standing." But King sat back down.

The soldier coughed and produced a letter, but did not hand it over.

"Sir, it is my grievous duty to inform you that your son William E. Cotton was killed in the line of duty serving our nation in Viet Nam."

"*Ay, Dios mio.*" Eloisa slumped into a chair.

"What did you say?"

"I'm so sorry, sir, your son's been killed in combat."

"Combat? Combat? Where? There ain't no war."

"Viet Nam, sir, Indochina."

"How can that be? His letters didn't say anything about being in this— this Viet Nam."

"Sir, none of our advisors there are at liberty to disclose their location, even to family members."

"Advisors." King's voice sounding to himself like it came from the recesses of a deep, distant cave.

The soldier's subsequent explanation about advisors was lost on him, as were Eloisa's loud sobs. The old man stared blankly ahead, lost in a fog of pain. The rest of the world was completely gone.

58

AFTER THE SOLDIER LEFT, KING went out to the back yard, short of breath and unable to reconcile himself to the news. "No, no. It can't be."

But he knew it was. He knew he had lost his son. He had lost his boy, his boy who was so handsome and so strong. The boy he'd pinned the family future on. Billy had it all. Looks, skill, popularity. He might have someday been a congressman or a senator if he'd gone to school instead of the Army.

Who was going to take care of the farm now, the many fields, the workers? Who would keep an eye on Jeff, Marcie? Who would carry on the family name, its rightful place among the valley's elite? The old man swayed where he stood, reached out for a picnic table for support.

He felt tired now, and old, so old. His head and chest hurt and his vision blurred. Then, all of a sudden, he felt light and his head cleared briefly. In that moment, he saw clouds and blue sky and wondered how he could be seeing them when he hadn't lifted his head. A sense of calm replaced the confusion and sadness, and he closed his eyes. His last thoughts were of Marcie and who would tell her about Billy.

Eloisa prided herself on respecting her *jefe's* privacy, but when he had not come back into the house after a quarter of an hour, she began to worry. She went to a back window and looked out. She could see most of the yard, but not him. She went to another window to see closer to the side of the house. About to give up, she spotted his big old boots, dirty as usual, off to one side of the picnic table. With a cry, she ran for the back door.

"Oh, no." She wept, rushing outside. *"Ave María, Dios mío, no.* Mr. King, Mr. King."

59

NEITHER JEFF NOR SHREVE HAD ever seen Marcie as business-like, or as caring, as she was in attending to her father. She was always at the old man's side and though he could neither move nor speak, she kept up a soothing, if one-sided, conversation with him.

"I don't think he can hear you." Shreve told her on one of his frequent visits to the bedside of his boss and benefactor. Jeff stood to one side, glowering at him.

"Nonsense." Marcie wiped King's forehead with a wet cloth. "You can hear just fine, can't you, Daddy? You're going to be well soon and back up and running the farm like always. Aren't you?"

"He won't ever do nothing again." Jeff frowned at Shreve. "If he don't get more rest and less people coming around bothering him."

Shreve matched Jeff's look, but said nothing. Marcie ignored them both.

"Does that feel better, Daddy?" She brushed back a stray lock of gray hair above the old man's left ear. She adjusted the sheet over him and fluffed the edge of his pillow.

Jeff and Shreve were locked in a staring contest.

"Ain't there somewhere you ought to be?" Jeff sneered.

"Where might that be?"

"Maybe in a whorehouse in Mexicali."

"Maybe I'd be shacked up with your girlfriend."

Jeff reached towards Shreve, who drew back and cocked his right arm. Marcie leapt up and threw herself between them.

"You stupid boys." She shoved them apart. "My father, the man who made both of you, is lying there. He can't even move, and you two are fighting like children. What is the matter with you?"

"This butthole started it."

"Butthole? I'll show you who's a butthole, you damn piss ant."

Marcie separated them again. "I don't give a damn who started it. You're both acting like fools. Now get out of here. Both of you. And I don't want to see either of you until you can act like grown men."

Shreve backed off. Jeff stood his ground. Marcie looked him dead in the eyes.

"Get out. I mean it."

He started to challenge her but instead stomped out with a haughty snort.

"Marcie."

"Don't, Shreve. Just go. Please."

"All right. I'll go. Good-bye." She turned back to attend to her father.

"Good-bye."

He stood there a moment longer, then went outside. Jeff was starting out of the driveway in his pickup but stopped when Shreve walked towards him.

"You got something more to say, Jeff?"

"Yeah, I got something to say. When the old man goes, boy, you go with him."

"We'll see about that."

"And we're gonna settle this between us one of these days, too."

"Any time." Shreve motioned with his hands for Jeff to get out of the pickup.

He spit out the window at Shreve's feet, then hit the gas and roared down the driveway in a cloud of dust, gravel spraying behind. Shreve stuck a middle finger up at the receding pickup.

"Butthole."

60

I T WAS BLUSTERY AND COLD out by the canals southwest of Cotton. As cold as Frank remembered it being in Cotton. He walked alone, carrying his .22. The wind gusted from side to side nearly knocking his baseball cap off. He had walked all the way out from town to go shooting, but he'd never even raised the weapon, much less fired it.

Head down into the gusts, he crossed a disked up field, watching his boots crunch the dusty soil. He was so intent on looking down, he nearly ran into a big tree at the end of the field. The tree was bare, permanently dead, not just dormant, and up on a small rise of soft dirt that provided a good windbreak. He jumped down in behind the tree and huddled against the earth protecting the tree's dying roots.

In the break, only occasional swirls of air could reach him, flipping stray locks of hair that stuck out from beneath his cap. He snuggled in against the dirt, resting his rifle across his legs. It felt warm there, a nice comfortable place out of the wind and cold. He sat still, almost dozing, resting, letting the events and changes of the past few months run freely through his mind.

So many people had died. Lar Turner, JFK, and now Billy Cotton, who he'd never even seen. Billy C., the very best, it was said, that Cotton had produced. Shot dead in some jungle in some country that no one hardly ever heard of before. And the old man, King, paralyzed by a stroke brought on by the news of his boy's death.

A dynasty, an age, an era was ending and the end had begun somehow with Billy's death. Or was it JFK's? Or Lar's? It was all mixed up. So many deaths so close together. They were all related somehow, although it wasn't clear why. Cates would have a theory about it and Richard an answer. Shreve would shake it all off and just keep going, keep on working.

Frank seldom saw his old friends anymore. Richard was far away at school in Oregon, Shreve was always working up in the north end, and Cates only came to VJC when he wasn't at his new job in El Centro.

Each had gone his separate way. But Frank had not. He imagined that he would have gone his own way like the others, except that he didn't know what his way was. It was coming to him, though, he could sense that, but he couldn't define it, or find it. Not just yet.

A big gust swirled into his hiding place, spraying dirt in his face. He pressed closer to the ground. Laying the rifle by his side, he rolled over toward it, resting his head on his left hand. The wind was blocked even more in this position and it got warmer again. He began to relax, to get sleepy. He blinked several times slowly, then closed his eyes. He sighed deeply and drifted off peacefully.

When he woke, yawning and adjusting his eyes to the light of the lengthening day, the wind had died down and it was sunny and bright. He looked up, surprised to see the sun well below its midday zenith. He must have dozed off for well over an hour, even more.

He rose slowly then, stiff-legged, and stretched. Inhaling and letting out a deep breath, he was surprised to find that he felt good again. The blue mood had passed with his relaxed nap. With a smile, he picked up his rifle and started walking back to town.

He was feeling good again now, not so down as when he had been considering all the troubling events of late, and more hopeful, more optimistic. The closer he got to town, the lighter his step became. After this much time away from Cotton, he figured he should get on home. Somebody might be wondering where he was.

61

ALITTLE BEFORE NOON ON the Saturday before Christmas, Shreve decided to go into Cotton just to see who was around. He made a couple of fruitless passes up and down Main, thinking of driving over to Brawley when he saw Cates coming out of Valley Hardware. He pulled up in front of the store.

"Hey, Cates."

"Well, what the hay." Cates pointed a long skinny arm at Shreve. "I thought you'd died and gone to Mexicali."

"No such luck. What you up to?"

"Just paying off a Christmas present."

"At the hardware? For your momma, huh?"

"Gimme a break."

"Wanna ride around some?"

"Heck, yes."

"Hop in."

Cates jumped in and they took off.

"Where's your Merc?"

"Over there in Manny's parking lot."

Shreve glanced over his shoulder. "Oh, I see it."

"So what you been up to, buddy?"

"Same old." They stopped at the intersection. "Just working. How 'bout you?"

"Same."

"It's been a while, huh?"

They went down Main past Jackson's Cafe, took a right and drove by some of the poorer homes over by the railroad tracks.

"Seems like a couple of months since I seen you." Cates watched a raggedy little kid playing in a junk-filled yard.

"Just about."

"I don't see Mason much either anymore, do you?"

"Must've been late summer or early in the fall."

"I only see him sometimes at school."

"The old gang's disappearing."

"Speaking of disappearing." They reached the north-south highway running through town. "Did ya hear old man Cole, the bum, just up and vanished?"

"I heard something. Maybe his little old shack burned?" Shreve turned right back toward downtown.

"Yeah, well, now the old man's gone."

"Jesus Christ, who's next? This town is coming apart at the seams."

"You ain't lying. Seems like everybody's dying, leaving, or disappearing into thin air."

"I hear you're moving to El Centro permanent yourself, is that right?"

"After Christmas."

"There you go, another one."

"You're staying, aren't you?"

"Oh, yeah. I won't be going nowhere."

"What about, Frankie? Think he'll be around much longer?"

"No way." Shreve pulled up to the south side of the four-way. "He'll be gone, sooner or later. Probably a lot sooner than later, if I know Mason."

"Yeah."

"Which way?" Cates looked right, then left.

"Left. Let's go by the park and the school. Maybe somebody else will be out."

"Okay."

But there was hardly anyone about, perhaps all gone to Brawley or El

Centro for last minute Christmas shopping. There were a couple of firemen in front of the station.

"Shreve, can I ask you a personal question?"

"Depends. But go ahead."

"Are you having a thing with Marcie Clayborn?"

"A thing?"

"You know, are you sleeping with her?"

"You're asking me if I'm sleeping with Marcie Clayborn, right now?" Shreve framed his question precisely.

"Yeah."

"No."

"Honest?"

"I said I wasn't, didn't I?"

"I'll be darned. I was sure you were."

Shreve didn't respond to Cates' disappointed tone, so they just drove around a while without talking. They made a loop by quiet Cotton High and headed back downtown.

"Well." Cates watched the fire station go by again. "I guess I better get on home. Family's all coming in, you know."

"I'll drop you off at Manny's."

"Say, did you hear about the train line they're going to put in between El Centro and LA?"

For the first time either of them could remember, Shreve let one of Cates' rumors go by without jumping on him or teasing him about it.

"No. I didn't hear about that."

"Well, yeah. Oh, hell, I never heard no such thing." Shreve pulled up behind the Mercury in Manny's lot. "All those stories are just bull, man. I make 'em up for the fun of it."

"Don't you think I know that, James?"

Cates chuckled as he opened the door and climbed out.

"Okay, buddy. We'll see you around."

"See you."

Cates shut the pickup door and walked away.

Shreve drove out the back of the lot and into the dirt alley behind Manny's.

The burnt remains of old Mr. Cole's house could still be seen off to the left. He turned right, drove to the highway, turned right again and pulled up to the four-way stop. Feeling relaxed and comfortable, he drove slowly through the intersection. A horn honked behind him and he looked in his mirror to see Cates turning at the intersection and heading toward his parents' home in Northland. He waved his left arm out the window.

Looking forward again, he was surprised to see Carol Scott up ahead on the right walking to town. He pulled over to the curb beside her. She wore blue jeans and a pullover sweater, her blonde hair hanging a little unkempt around her shoulders.

"Hi, Carol."

"Hi."

He thought she looked especially nice this day. Sweet and kind of tired, vulnerable somehow and a lot more grown up than she used to seem.

"How are you doing?"

"Fine."

"Would you like to go to Brawley and get something to eat?"

"I guess so."

"You don't have to. Were you going somewhere else?"

"Oh, no, I was just taking a walk."

"Sure?"

"Sure, I'm sure. That would be real nice."

He leaned over and pushed the door open for her. She climbed in beside him, her glance perhaps carrying the hint of some promise.

"It's a nice day to go for a drive."

"It's a nice day to go anywhere." She shut the door.

Shreve shifted into first and pulled back out on the road. He drove slowly out of town. There was no reason to be in a hurry.

62

I T'S TOO BAD YOU GOTTA work tonight, Mom. Of all nights."

"It's just for a couple of hours." Kate put on a jacket. "I'll be back by nine. Poor Wanda needs a little time with her family, too." They heard a horn honk on the street below the apartment. "That'll be your Uncle Carl."

"See you at their place later."

"Okay. Aunt Jean'll have cookies and eggnog, so go over whenever you want."

"All right."

"Try to enjoy yourself, son. After all, it is Christmas Eve."

"Okay, Mom."

"Bye-bye."

"Bye."

Left alone, Frank sat around the apartment listening to the radio and thumbing through a worn out copy of *Boys' Life*. The magazine that he once loved seemed overly childish and silly to him now and he tossed it down.

No matter how hard he tried to avoid it, a nameless sense of dissatisfaction and emptiness kept reasserting itself over his desire to be happy. Even the small, cheerfully decorated Christmas tree failed to lift his spirits. He couldn't stop feeling like something was gone or that something had been lost that he could never get back.

He got up and went out to the closet in the hall where he'd stashed a bottle of Mexicali-bought vodka behind the hot water heater. He opened the bottle, started to take a drink, then screwed the cap back on and hid the bottle away again. The hallway was completely still. The other two apartments, where the old guy had died the year before and Preacher Wilcox had lived before he disappeared, were empty and silent.

He went back into the apartment and opened the refrigerator. Nothing looked good. Grabbing a light sweater, he turned off the radio and lights and went out. Maybe on the street he'd run into Cates or somebody and they could hang out a while.

Outside, the streets of Cotton on Christmas Eve were completely deserted. The air was crisp but not cold, so he decided to stand on the corner a while and see if any big trucks would come blasting through town on a last minute Christmas run. After a quarter of an hour, the streets were still empty.

He walked around the corner and took the back steps up to the roof of the apartment. From there he had a panoramic view of Cotton with its flagpole decorated for all the valley to see. He saw the community church and beyond it Annie Bishop's house. Closer to his right was the burnt out shell of old Mr. Cole's house and below—Main Street, a gray concrete path leading out of town to the west, into the dark toward the Cotton ranch.

Out there they would still be mourning the death of their son and brother. He tried to picture Billy Cotton dead in some jungle in Indochina, but he couldn't. Instead, he recalled Cates' joke about shooting Billy C. the night they went chasing around town looking for him. At the time, the joke seemed funny, now it was painfully ironic.

He huddled in his sweater. On an impulse, he looked up at the black sky with its first stars beginning to appear and then, in a flash of insight, he understood that this would be his last Christmas in Cotton. His time in the little town had come and gone.

Some new age might be at hand, as he suspected, but he wouldn't see it arrive in Cotton. He didn't know where he might go—there was still another semester of junior college remaining—but he knew he would be gone, and soon. Maybe he would go back home to the Ozarks. Doubtful. Most likely he would enlist in the service. He didn't know for sure.

Pulling the sweater tight around his chest, he went back down the stairs to the sidewalk. Cotton was dead quiet. He walked up to the four-way stop. A piece of scrap paper blew by, flitting back and forth at the mercy of the wind. It was so quiet he went out into the middle of the street and stood motionless facing south.

He remained there a long, quiet, thoughtful moment. Finally he stirred, looked left, then right. After another pause he turned left, to the east, and slowly moved on through the center of town. He wasn't sure where he was headed. He was just walking.

J.B. HOGAN IS A PROLIFIC and award-winning author. He grew up in Fayetteville, Arkansas, but moved to Southern California in 1961 before entering the U. S. Air Force in 1964. After the military, he went back to college, receiving a Ph.D. in English from Arizona State University in 1979.

J.B. has published over 250 stories and poems. His novels, *The Apostate, Tin Hollow, Time and Time Again: The Curious Case of Mr. Stephen White,* and *Mexican Skies*—as well as his local baseball history book, *Angels in the Ozarks,* a short story collection entitled *Fallen,* and his book of poetry, *The Rubicon*—are available at Amazon, iBooks, Barnes & Noble, Books-A-Million, and Walmart.

When he's not writing or teaching, J.B. plays upright bass in East of Zion, a family band specializing in bluegrass-flavored Americana music, and is active in the Washington County (AR) Historical Society, where he's recently served as President.

www.thejbhogan.com

www.ingramcontent.com/pod-product-compliance
Lightning Source LLC
Chambersburg PA
CBHW020632180626
46816CB00003B/934